CRY

of the

GOLDEN

WOLF

I0678539

Other Books by
Christopher Fahy

Novels:
Belief
Farnswell
Winterhill
Foreverglades
Gone from the Game
The Christmas Star
Red Tape
Chasing the Sun
Breaking Point
Fever 42
The Fly Must Die
The Lyssa Syndrome
Eternal Bliss
Dream House
Nightflyer
The Compost Heap

Short Stories:
Matinee at the Flame
Limerock: Maine Stories
Greengroundtown

Poetry:
The Toast of Paris
My Life in Water
The End Beginning

Nonfiction:
Society Hill
Home Remedies

CRY

of the

GOLDEN

WOLF

Christopher Fahy

Cry of the Golden Wolf

Cover and Art Design
Cortney Skinner

Formatting by Nina Pierce of Seaside Publications
ninapierce.com/book-formatting

ISBN: 978-0-9637727-7-0

Limerock Books
15 Mechanic Street • Thomaston ME 04861
limebks@gmail.com

For Davene, Greg, Ben

CAROL

GRAMMY HASTINGS WAS DEAD. Carol looked through the windshield, watching the naked trees and dull gray sky flow past and thought: Dead. *Dead. At last.*

Her husband, Tony, touched the brake and the car wound down the ramp and away from Route One. Carol glanced at the back seat, where Robbie, her eight-year-old, was sitting stiffly next to Lillian, Tony's older sister, who stared straight ahead as if hypnotized, her thin face sad and drawn. Good God, Carol thought. They're sick, and I feel like dancing.

And why not? For thirteen years she'd catered to Grammy's iron will for the sake of Tony and Robbie, making concessions, holding her feelings in check, and now the long struggle was over. She felt as if she'd been freed from a long stay in jail. Amazing the power that woman had wielded right up until three days ago. And then, after all those years of scheming and clawing, she'd gone up to bed and had never come down again. Like Alexander the Great, Carol thought. Like Napoleon.

Gone, at the age of eighty-four. No more of her carping, her picking, her sour snide comments. "The potatoes aren't the way *I* would have made them, Carol, but I guess they'll do." "It's not the sort of pattern one *ought* to have in a parlor, it's much better suited to a bedroom." No matter how hard Carol tried, she could never please Grammy Hastings. But now, praise God, she no longer had to try.

Who at the funeral would really be sad? she asked herself. Tony, Lillian, Robbie, yes. But Victor? Ruth? Not on your life. Who in that sparse collection that followed the hearse would truly be sorry that Grammy had cashed in her chips? The chips were all they really cared about. This thought made Carol laugh inside at Grammy's last bitter joke.

Tony stepped on the gas and shot into the flow of the West Arterial traffic, jolting his sister Lillian out of her stupor. "Tony! Don't go so fast!"

Tony took a long drag on his cigarette. "It's okay, Lil, everything's under control."

Ah yes, Carol thought, all's under control. His mother's death had hit him hard, but as always he showed the world nothing.

"Watch the car on your right!" said Lillian, and Carol thought, *Shut up.*

"I see it, Lil."

"Well then act like you see it."

"You bet, Lil.

Carol sighed and looked over at Robbie, whose eyelid twitched. His stomach had hurt this morning and he'd eaten no breakfast, and yet he'd insisted on coming today—had been quite adamant about it. Two years ago when his grandmother's younger brother Frank had died they hadn't let him attend the funeral, but nevertheless the death had obsessed him for weeks. Now he was almost nine, and if he wanted to go to the funeral of his beloved Grammy, how could they say no?

Carol said, "How's it going, Rob?"

He kept staring outside. "Pretty good."

"How's your stomach?"

"Okay."

He chewed on his lip and Carol thought: a mystery. Just like his father, a mystery. I love them both dearly, but *understand* them?

Lillian was scowling. "Tony, *must* you smoke? Can't you wait till we get to the parking lot? If you want to kill yourself, it's up to you, but don't take *me* along."

Tony rolled down the window; cold air rushed in. He flipped his cigarette onto the highway and rolled up the window again.

"And it's bad for Robbie's stomach, too—not to mention his lungs."

"Lil—it's gone."

"Well turn on the ventilation, it's awful in here."

Tony did as directed. A soft whirring sound, a cool breeze, and the smell of smoke died. Then a sniffling began, and Lillian daubed at her eyes with her handkerchief. "She's gone," she said. "I still can't believe it, that dear Mother is gone."

"Eighty-four years old," Tony said with a shrug. "We should all be so lucky. She had a good life."

His sister nodded. At forty-six, her hair was completely gray. "Yes, she did. Never sick. Then it happened so fast." She sobbed into her linen hanky and Robbie squirmed.

"Lil," Tony said.

In her mind's eye Carol saw Grammy again; thin, hard, severe and dressed in black, her sharp eyes condemning all they fell upon—except Tony and Robbie and Lil. She had doted on Robbie, her only grandchild, and Robbie had gone along with her ministrations—all too well, Carol thought. Spending hours in that gloomy upstairs room at Grammy's huge Victorian house, that library filled with those wacky books on psychic healing and ESP and that oddball stuff on the shelves: old amulets, exotic shells from Brazil, a raccoon skull, an ancient, polished revolver, and her figurines: a unicorn, a ballet dancer, a soldier with a sword, a monkey with a little red hat, and Robbie's favorite, a windup ice truck holding a driver and tiny silver cubes of ice. Then every so often she'd show him that cane with the solid gold head of a wolf she would let no one touch. The whole scene gave Carol the creeps.

And to top it all off, that raven. Good old Grip, its banded leg chained to its stand. The damned thing had nipped Robbie's thumb one time when he got too close, but that hadn't stopped him from seeing Grammy. A child's love for his grandmother, usually normal enough, but in this case somehow unhealthy, Carol thought. God only knew what kinds of weird notions the woman had put into Robbie's head. Well, Carol thought, no more.

Tony and Lillian stood in the parking lot. Tony was smoking again, looking off at the pines behind the church as his sister stared at the grass with twitching eyes. A shaft of pallid November sun fought its way through the clouds, then died.

"Do you want to wait here in the car?" Carol asked, and Robbie said, "No, I want to come in."

"Then let's go."

They left the car and Carol locked the door.

Tony sucked at the last of his cigarette, ground it under his foot, exhaled, and the four of them started toward the chapel. The sign beside its door said, FIRST SPIRIT CHURCH OF MAINE. As Tony always said, "First and Only." He and his older brother had gone to this church with their mother until they were on their own, when they quit religion, but Lillian held fast to their mother's beliefs.

Robbie calmed himself by sniffing his right hand's fingertips, though Carol hated him doing that. He took his hand away from his face and looked at his shoes. They were shiny and black and hurt his toes. Aunt Lillian had bought them for him.

The sun broke through again and the wind kicked up, and Lillian clutched the front of her coat as they all went up the steps and into the mudroom.

It was warm and dark inside. Victor, the oldest of Grammy's three children at fifty and Ruth, forty-eight, his wife, were already there and quietly said hello. Organ music played in the background, watery and soft. The funeral director, rosy, plump Mr. Bachman, came over and shook their hands. Well fed, Carol thought, on the blood of the dead.

Mr. Bachman lined everyone up and pinned black ribbons on their lapels. Carol watched as Robbie touched his gingerly, adjusting it, then inspected his fingers. To see if the black had come off?

Mr. Bachman, raising his eyebrows, asked, "This is all the immediate family?"

Victor said that it was, and Bachman said, "We're ready to begin then, follow me."

As they walked behind him, the music grew louder. He stopped, parted a brown velvet curtain, and nodded. They went through the curtain and into the light. Carol fumbled for Robbie's hand. It felt hot and small.

As she entered the chapel her breath seemed to stick in her throat. Robbie's hand tightened and anger flashed through her. "Lillian," she whispered, "you promised!"

Lillian's wrinkled eyelids fluttered. She looked straight ahead—where Grammy Hastings, all in white, lay on white silk in an open casket.

"You promised me the casket would be closed!"

Lillian ignored her.

Carol was fuming. Just what she didn't want her son to be exposed to, and now it was too late.

The dead woman looked incredibly small to Carol. Had the loss of her spirit shrunken her? Or perhaps the embalming process? So tiny. Or maybe the white dress was to blame, she had always worn black…

Black! What was that black near her head? Good God, it was Grip, her raven! It had died the day after Grammy died, but whose idea was this? Lillian's again?

Carol looked down at Robbie. He was staring at Grammy's puckered mouth, her fastened eyes. Her withered, craggy cheeks had an odd rose blush to them. Carol wanted to strangle Lillian. How dare she subject them to this?

Robbie started to sniff the fingers of his free hand. "Please don't do that," his mother said.

The organ music pulsed through Carol's veins. Pale light filtered into the chapel through amber glass. The pews were practically empty. Grammy had not been a sociable person and the few friends she'd had were dead or in nursing homes.

Victor and Ruth had taken their turn at the casket and Lillian stood there now. She bowed her head and closed her eyes and folded her bony hands. Time seemed suspended. Carol thought, For God's sake, Lillian, hurry up! She stared at the raven on the pillow. Its feathers looked shiny, waxed, as Grammy Hastings herself looked waxed, her white hair lacquered and stiff.

Lillian was mouthing something, taking forever, and Carol glanced to her left. A heavy, bizarre-looking woman with a yellow turban and huge gold earrings sat in the second row. Who in the world is *that*? Carol wondered, and felt Robbie's hand slip away.

To her shock, she saw that Lillian had her arm around his shoulders. She heard her say in a low voice, "Step up close. Step up and give Grammy a kiss."

"No!" Carol whispered. Heat rushed to her face.

"Step up and kiss Grammy goodbye."

Robbie stared at the coffin, the shrunken white head. His pale face bloomed with sweat. "Grip," he said.

"Let him go!" Carol whispered, and Lillian squinted at her.

"Stop making a scene! The child should have a right to a proper goodbye!" And turning to Robbie again she said, "Kiss her! Grammy loves you, she wants your kiss. It's the last chance you'll get, very soon she'll be gone forever. Do it, Robbie! Now!"

"Lillian!"

Robbie's face was just inches away from the corpse. Its hair had a silvery shine that wasn't right and its skin was powdery, thick. Another wrong thing was the eye closest to him, its crooked lid. He could see a slit of eyeball through it, milky and dull, and it seemed to be watching. It was like she was only pretending death and could see him hesitating...

"Quickly, Robbie, don't keep her waiting, she loves you, you must, you owe it to her—"

His lips touched the powdered dead cheek. He expected the flesh to be cold, but no, it was hot, it burned, and he jumped back quickly and put his hand over his mouth.

Carol gasped.

"Good, Robbie," Lillian said. "Grammy's proud of you, now let's sit down."

"She's hot," Robbie said.

"Let's take our seats."

"Her face was hot."

"Here, take my hand."

"Take *mine*," Carol whispered between clenched teeth. "I'll never forgive you, Lillian, you promised—" Her throat closed off. She was almost in tears.

"Carol, please," said Lillian with a scowl. "Show respect for the dead."

The pastor said, "We believe that the spirit survives the change called death. We affirm that communication with the dead is factual."

Robbie sat transfixed. The coffin was closed now, its ebony surface dull in the lambent light, but Robbie could still see Grammy in his mind, with Grip beside her on the silk. Remembering the kiss, he ran his tongue across his tingling lips then wiped them on his sleeve. "As spiritualists, we believe…" The pastor's voice seemed weak and far away.

He watched his father and Uncle Victor and four other men he didn't know lug the coffin outside, slide it into the long black car. Then he got in the car with his father, mother, aunt and a man in a black raincoat. The man drove.

"Inexcusable," Carol said.

Aunt Lillian said, "It's the way that we did it when I was a girl, it's the proper way."

"It's barbaric."

"You never liked Mother."

"Don't try to divert me," Carol said. "We had an agreement."

"Okay, everybody, what's done is done," Tony said.

"So you're supporting her?"

"Nope. I'm just tired of hearing this stuff."

Lillian scowled. Her thin lips twitched. "As if it would harm the child," she said, and looked at Robbie. "You're fine, aren't you, Robbie?"

"I'm fine," Robbie echoed.

"See, Carol, I told you."

"Hey Lil," Tony said, "that's enough, okay?" He looked out the window. "Good grief, is that snow? On November the eighth? Maine or no Maine, that's weird."

They were silent the rest of the way.

Sparse silvery flakes swirled over the gathering, frosting the dark green grass. Robbie stood with his mother up front. The wind caught the pastor's Bible, fluttered the pages, carrying his words away. The canopy over the coffin rippled and flapped. The pastor soon closed his book and the box was descending.

Lillian tossed gladiolas at it, her cheeks streaked with tears. Carol watched her, numb. What a waste of good flowers, she thought. Down and down the coffin sank—and Robbie began to wheeze.

Carol turned to him quickly. "Rob?"

That all too familiar look on his face, his dark eyes staring, his mouth open wide. "Can't breathe," he said. His right hand clutched his coat.

"You'll be all right," Carol said.

"I can't—" His eyes bulged and his mouth fought for air.

She grabbed his hand and pulled him back from the group. He wheezed and turned red as she searched her purse. "Here we go," she said, and uncapped the bottle and poured a spoonful of liquid.

He opened his mouth and swallowed hard. Gagged, looked as if he might retch. He was breathing heavily, eyes darting, his hand at his throat.

The two of them stood in silence, snow coating their hair. Robbie's breathing slowed down. His complexion returned to normal. The graveside gathering was breaking up, so they started to walk toward the hearse.

"Feeling better?"

"Yeah."

"It worked fast this time."

He looked at her. "What?"

"The medicine."

He frowned. "Oh, yeah."

Funny kid, Carol thought. The asthma was real, but he was a hypochondriac, a worry wart—the total opposite of his dad, but just as much of a mystery. "You feel okay?" she asked.

He simply shrugged.

The wake was at Victor and Ruth's. Their house was five times as big as Carol's and could hold a substantial crowd, but there was no crowd, just a handful of people scattered about. Carol knew a few of them but Tony seemed to know them all. "Who's that with the turban?" Carol asked and he said, "Oh, Mother's medium, Mrs. Carney. A fortune teller. You know those spiritualists…"

Lillian sat in a stiff-backed chair in the dining room and picked at a crustless triangular sandwich, frowning at the kitchen, where Tony stuffed himself and chattered away. He'd worked as a real estate agent for years and talked about various places for sale. His patter was smooth as soft butter. "Diapers, divorce and death, that's the key, all right." "That big Victorian over on Fifth? Funny you asked about that…"

Robbie sat on the huge white living room couch, eating and drinking nothing. Carol brought him a ginger ale and he took two tiny sips, then put it down.

Shortly after five o'clock, Carol took Tony aside and said, "We'd better get on the road."

Tony's face was bright. Ashes fell from his cigarette, splashed onto his shirt. "What's the hurry?" he said. "I haven't seen some of these people in years, and the snow stopped long ago."

"Lillian's restless and Robbie's wiped out."

"Give me fifteen more minutes, I want to ask Vic about something."

"Ask Vic about what?"

"Just something."

"A loan."

He grinned. "A loan? Wouldn't think of it, sweetheart."

When they finally left an hour later, Tony was plastered and Carol drove. Robbie sat in the back seat, his aunt beside him. "What a marvelous human being," she said. "Raising three children alone as she did, the brilliant way she managed her investments… A great person."

Tony was snoring, dead to the world, his hands interlaced on his bulging stomach. "A very strong person," Carol said, and thought: but don't ask me to say she was great.

"You miss your Grammy, don't you, Robbie?" Lillian said. "Well, we were good to her. We went to church every Sunday and prayed for her soul and afterwards went to see her."

Robbie frowned. "Why did God kill her," he said, "even when we prayed for her?"

Lillian sniffed. "Everyone has to die, Robbie, you know that. I'll die, you'll die, your mother and father—"

From the driver's seat Carol said, "Lillian, please."

"All God's creatures must die, that's a part of God's plan. And a wonderful plan it is."

"Well how come she took Grip with her?"

"She loved Grip, Robbie. And Grip loved Grammy so much that once she was dead, he also died."

"I was her friend, am I going to die?"

Carol thought: *my God.*

"Of course not," Lillian said. "You're young and Grip was old." She laughed in her dry, tight way. "I guess you miss her terribly."

"Not really," Robbie said.

This response startled Carol. Lillian said, "Of course you do, you loved her very much, and now you miss her."

"Well…"

"You do."

"Well, yes, but…"

"What?"

"Not really. Not a lot."

"What a contrary child you are at times," said Lillian. She glanced at her dozing brother. "As the twig is bent, the tree's inclined, I suppose."

Carol braked, turned the corner, pulled up to the curb beside Lillian's car. She was tired in every bone. "All right, Lillian, here we are." Tony jerked and his head rolled back.

Lillian grabbed her purse and opened the door. She stepped outside then leaned back in again, took Robbie's hand in hers and said, "The Lord can cure you, Robbie, always believe it. Pray to him, Robbie, pray tonight, say Jesus, dear Jesus, erase this horrible curse that the devil has visited on me. Allow me to breathe your pure air without hindrance, to smell the flowers of your fields—"

"Lillian," Carol said, "good night!"

"And say a prayer for Grammy's spirit," Lillian babbled on. "A prayer for that shining spirit that rests in heaven now, the spirit of Grammy Hastings, who you miss *so much* and will never see again." She lowered her voice to a whisper and said, "You did the right thing when you kissed her, Robbie. She'll love you forever, you did the *right* thing."

"Lillian!"

Tony snorted and opened his eyes. His sister straightened up and said, "Thank you, Carol, for the ride. I'll see you Sunday, Robbie. Good night."

"Night, Lil," Tony mumbled, then lapsed into sleep again.

Carol drove into the garage and she and Robbie got out of the car. Tony didn't move. Carol opened his door and said, "We're home."

Tony yawned and sputtered, stumbled out of the car and said, "Jesus, it snowed." He staggered toward the mudroom door. Once inside, he clapped his hand on Carol's shoulder, looked at her with bloodshot eyes and said, "A great woman. I know you never liked her, but she was great."

"I liked her more than she liked *me*," Carol said.

"Not true," Tony said. He took off his coat and hung it up on one of the mudroom's pegs, put his hat there too, wavered a little, fell back a step. "I'm bushed," he said with a little laugh, then kissed Carol's forehead and went upstairs.

Robbie's face was pale. He hated to see his father this way, just hated it. His mother said, "Do you want to eat something, Rob?"

He shook his head. "No thanks."

"All that food at Uncle Victor's and you didn't touch a crumb."

"I wasn't hungry."

"You didn't eat all day. Not even breakfast."

"It wasn't a day for eating."

Carol drew him to her, held him, rubbed his hair. "It's hard," she said. "Losing someone you love is the hardest thing in the world."

"I feel okay about it now."

"No more stomach pains?"

"No."

"Then why don't you eat something? PB and J?"

"No thanks."

"You can't get big if you never eat."

"Uh-huh. Mom? How come you didn't like Grammy?"

"I liked her well enough."

"But not really."

"Carol sighed. We'll talk about this some other time."

"Okay. I'm tired, I'm going up. Come on, Tofu."

Tofu was Robbie's cat, part Siamese, part alley. The pediatrician, Dr. Janes, said it might help his asthma to get rid of her, but Robbie would never do that.

His mother kissed his head. "Good night. And pleasant dreams."

"Thanks, Mom." He hesitated. "Mom?"

"What, Rob?"

"Do ravens have spirits?"

"According to your Aunt Lillian they do, but according to most other people they don't."

"Oh," Robbie said.

He went to the bathroom and brushed his teeth. His lips still felt funny, tingly and warm. He thought of the kiss he had given Grammy and rinsed his mouth again.

He got into bed with Tofu, turned off the light and lay on his back, staring up at the ceiling. When he closed his eyes, bright images flooded his mind: the brooding sky, the spitting snow, the casket, Grammy's wrinkled face. When his lips touched her cheek and he felt that sudden shocking heat, he thought: Dead people should be cold!

He remembered the casket going down into the hole and the feeling that he was also going down, the darkness was closing in on him forever and ever. That terrible tension in his chest, a giant hand squeezing his lungs and driving out all the air, he couldn't breathe…

Aunt Lillian had said, "You miss your Grammy, Don't you?" and he'd said, "Not really," but he hadn't told her why. *Because she isn't really dead!* he'd thought. *Her spirit is still alive!*

Turning onto his side now, frowning and clutching his penis as he often did when he prayed, he whispered into the empty dark, "Dear God, please let there be no life after death. Please. *Please!*

JEFF

IT WAS JUST AFTER two a.m. Jeff Harris removed his glasses, set them down on the littered desktop, fingered his beard, then covered his eyes with his hands.

A thin whine rang in his ears. *Enough*, he told himself. He took his hands away, put his glasses back on, and stared at the last page he'd typed.

Discouraged, he looked at the ashtray filled with butts, at the half empty Marlboro pack, at the two empty Pepsi bottles. The next section was starting to chatter, shaping itself. Past that, in the shadows beyond the halo of light cast off by his brass floor lamp, lay the rest of the book: an ocean, dark and undulating.

After days of this self-imposed isolation, he was starting to talk to himself and he said aloud, "Sorry, you'll have to wait, I'll deal with you tomorrow. Good night."

But he looked at the last page of what he had written again. "No, not good night, not yet," he said, getting up from his black leather chair. "I'll be back."

Since dinner at six (such as it was, a bowl of vegetable soup and a slice of bread) he'd had nothing to eat. Two Pepsis and four cigarettes and not a speck of food in seven hours, and he was starving. At one point, somewhere around eleven, he'd almost stopped for a snack, but as soon as he started to rise from his chair the story had pulled him back and he'd lit up another cigarette and hunched down over the keys again, and his hunger was lost in those last two pages; over and over again he reworked them, changing the order, changing the dialogue, until finally they seemed right.

Or almost right, he said to himself as he stood there looking at them. As usual, almost right.

He walked through the tiny living room, past the ancient couch, the wall that was lined with books, the full-length mirror, the dying woodstove (the cabin's only source of heat), and entered the kitchen. He turned on the overhead light—a bright fluorescent, which made him wince—and crossed to the refrigerator. "And your nightcap, as always, will be a nice glass of milk," he said, as he opened the door and removed the carton, "for you are a good boy now." He sniffed, took a glass from the shelf above the sink, set it down on the counter, and poured it half full. More than that and he'd piss all night, what with those two measly Pepsis. That's what it meant to be fifty-nine. That and a pair of reading specs and a pain in the shoulder that left in the morning but came back at night in his sleep.

Chocolate chip cookies sat in a bag near the stove. He took out three of them and ate distractedly, his mind still wrapped up in the story. If he were the man he'd like to be, he'd go back to that study and write straight through for days.

He'd heard, but never quite believed, that some writers worked that way. Not him. After four or five hours his writing would turn to mush. He had to rest, conserve himself, always keeping the fire banked, not letting it die, guarding the burning coals even in sleep, then finding the strength, day after day, to fan them white hot again, if only for an hour or two.

Tonight he had worked much longer than usual. It was one of those wonderful moments he had sometimes, especially at the start of a book, when he didn't know what he was into yet. On some of the nights that lay ahead he would work much less; would wonder if he could even continue, things would look so bleak. But most of the time his thoughts would come into the clear again, and eventually he would finish. And if he had luck, what he wrote would be good.

He ate all the cookies and milk, realizing he'd hardly tasted them. Typical when he was working: the real world practically ceased to exist. He had never been able to explain this to Allison no matter how hard he tried, and with Sandra he didn't push it. So hard to explain to a person who never got caught in the fictional trance. They said they understood what you meant by that trance, then held it against you, resented you for it.

A wonderful night, but his mind was spinning. He rinsed out his glass, left it there in the stainless-steel sink. "Hit the sack, for god's sake," he told himself, "or you'll have nothing left for tomorrow."

He decided to go outside for a minute and breathe the icy air, it would help him sleep. No jacket, he wanted to feel the cold. He closed the kitchen door behind him, walked to the path that led down to the river and stood looking up at the stars. After a couple of minutes of this, chilled to the bone, he went back inside, put more wood in the airtight stove and turned the damper down.

The cabin was fine, just what he needed. It had a tiny kitchen, bathroom, living room and two small bedrooms, one of which he used as his study. At first he'd been skeptical about staying alone in these woods but then he'd warmed to the idea. He thought of Montaigne in his tower, Thoreau in his hut. No one would bother him here, he'd have complete peace and quiet. He had plenty of food in the freezer and on the shelves so he didn't need to go anywhere. As long as the electric didn't fail, he would be all set.

Sandra had helped him move in. "Not as bad as I pictured it," she said. She lived in the city not far from him, two hours away from here, and might come by every now and again with treats and to see how he was holding up, but other than that, nobody—unless someone wanted to walk to the river, which very few people cared to do this time of the year.

He'd decided to grow a beard. He'd shaved all his life, but what was the point of that now? He wasn't going to see anybody except for Sandra every so often, so what was the point of wasting his time with shaving? The growth was heavy with gray, of course—well, actually white—and made him look older. Sandra would be surprised to see him this way.

He had met Sandra in AA. Her husband, Larry, had suddenly died of a heart attack eight years ago, leaving her to bring up two young girls by herself. Devastated by his death, she had started to drink. With time it began to get out of hand, and she needed help. Jeff was already in the group, having drunk way too much after he split with Allison. He and Sandra hit it off and it turned out she lived in a house only ten blocks away from his apartment and they saw each other a lot—went to dinners and plays and walks in the woods and grew fond of each other. Very fond.

Sandra was great: attractive, kind, smart, with a good sense of humor—and the reason he'd come to this place. His editor, Don Leonard, hadn't especially liked the last book he wrote but agreed to publish it anyway because of Jeff's track record, which was solid. Not spectacular, but solid. Sales of this one, as Don had predicted, were disappointing, to say the least. As a matter of fact, they had been so bad that Jeff worried his publisher might not do another book of his.

Sandra hadn't liked this book as much as his other ones either; she agreed with Don that it was repetitious, and encouraged Jeff to shake himself up, try something different. Something spooky, maybe.

"People loved to be scared," she said.

"You're right," he said, "though god knows why, life is scary enough as it is."

"Maybe a mystery, then."

"I can't stand mysteries, they're all the same. All these suspects to keep you guessing and then…"

"But that's what readers like about them."

"And what I hate about them."

"A fantasy story?"

"You mean castles and dragons and armor-clad armies? Spare me!"

"Not that kind of stuff, something on a small domestic scale."

He shrugged. "I don't know. It's something to think about."

Maybe a change of venue would help, she said. He hadn't wanted to move to her house since her younger daughter, Becky, was still around, but if he'd get out of his tiny apartment and go somewhere different…

"It sounds intriguing, but…"

"I think it would do you good," she said, "and I have a spot in mind. One of Larry's old friends has a rustic cabin about two hours from here which he only uses in the summer. I'll look into it."

She did. And of course she could use it, the old friend said—for free. All she needed to do was keep it up and pay the electric bill.

So now here Jeff was with no radio, no TV, no phone or internet. He'd put the real world on hold for his fictional world. To write, he'd gone back to his portable Smith Corona. At first it was weird, but now it was good.

During the first few days of this regimen, he'd felt severely deprived. He missed the bustle of the city. And no newscasts, no emails, no phone calls… He was restless and empty. Had another quake struck San Francisco? Was an asteroid on track to pulverize the earth? Had somebody shot the President? And, most importantly, had the Patriots beaten the Jets? But then he'd adapted and now he thought: Who cares?

"Go to bed!" he told himself again, but the last page of what he had written kept nagging him. Okay, I'll check it one more time, he thought, and walked back to the study.

He'd decided to try a fantasy. He'd never done something

like that before and he didn't have a real handle on it yet but it seemed to be moving in a good direction. He sat in his chair, leaned forward, picked up the troublesome page, then said to himself, "Oh no."

He saw a small dot in his vision, a small blank space—the start of a visual migraine. He'd had them for fifteen years. They started out with tiny specks and quickly spread to jagged yellow-green rings and blind spots in both eyes. The rings and blindness kept expanding until after twenty minutes or so they disappeared and his vision was whole again. For an hour or more after that, however, things seemed distorted, part of an off-kilter world that gradually restored its former shape at energy's expense: he was often quite tired, and sometimes he had a headache. On rare occasions his hands or one side of his face would go numb, and he had trouble speaking. And sometimes his fingers would tremble.

Regular migraines, the kind where you had to withdraw to a dark quiet room because of the sickness and pain, often diminished with the years. But visual migraines kept getting worse in frequency—and often in intensity.

The first time he had one he thought he was going blind or having a stroke and so did the ER doctor. But the symptoms soon faded, so nothing disastrous like that. He went to his ophthalmologist then, who made the right call: visual migraine.

There was nothing to do but wait the damn things out, there was no cure. In all the years they'd plagued him he'd never found a way to modify them, let alone short circuit them. He'd gone to two neurologists, but they'd been no help. An electrical brain event called "cortical spreading depression," they'd said, and he just had to wait till the symptoms passed. He was able to clean, cook, mow the lawn, etc. while they progressed, but found it impossible to read or write.

But now he was worried. He'd experienced more and more of them over the last few months and they'd taken a troublesome turn. After the light show stopped, he would notice a grainy quality in his eyes' periphery, something like a window screen, and at the far edges a shimmering that—on his right—took various shapes: a dog, a tree, a truck, and recently—it had come several times—a man.

He sat there thinking about what he had written as the flashing controlled his head. He just wanted to sleep, but he couldn't while the show continued. Migraines were always extremely annoying, but why did one have to happen *now*?

He thought of the part in his book where the boy clutched his penis. He sighed, leaned back, and shook his head. "Don won't let me keep it," he said aloud to the empty room. "I know he won't."

"Just tell him you're *going* to keep it."

He jumped so hard the chair made a small screeching sound on the bare wood floor.

He hadn't said that! Or had he? Had he actually said that aloud?

The flashing had pretty much died, but this was something new. An *auditory* hallucination, and now at the edge of his vision he saw that man, and thought: *I'm cracking up.* No, no, I just need sleep! "But how—"

"I'm your friend," said the voice.

Jeff shot up from the chair. His heart was beating wildly now, he was starting to sweat. The migraine was into its final throes, but the man was still there. Jeff blinked several times and took a deep breath.

He staggered into the bedroom, fell onto the bed and stared at the ceiling. Little pinwheels of yellow, migraine remnants, but no voice now, no man. Thank god. But I can't continue to write this late, he thought, it's doing weird things to me.

The pinwheels dissolved and he turned off the bedside lamp. Calm down, he told himself, just an aberration, it may never happen again.

He was drifting to sleep when the voice came back. "Don't think you'll escape from me," it said.

A chill went through him. His breath was thick. He stayed awake for another hour, staring up. No more voice. He slept but not well, worried he'd hear it again, so real, as if it was outside his head. But the only voices he heard were the regular voices we all hear constantly every day, all the time, just regular thoughts.

He was up at ten and didn't feel too bad in spite of the lack of sleep. He was sure that the migraine had caused the voice. No migraines, no man, no voice. But he couldn't prevent the migraines.

They came in clusters. He'd have a few for a week or so— what he called a "migrainous state"—might go for a couple of months without one, think he might be done with them, and then they'd start again. One time he had six in a row and was thoroughly wrecked with a vicious headache. That was two years ago, and it never happened again.

But they came more frequently now and this grainy vision and shimmering man was new. And the voice was *very* new—and frightening. He wondered if his brain was disintegrating. What were the early symptoms of that, and did you recognize them? Did you *know* you were going crazy? Or was this just something *others* knew? Was it hell? Or heaven? Did the affected person *like* it? He had a friend who'd begun seeing visions and hearing voices saying that Elvis, back from the dead, was out to kill him. He was given a lot of drugs but finally had to be put in an institution. "Don't think about that!" Jeff said.

Sandra knew about his migraines, of course. He'd had to pull over several times while he was driving with her to wait for them to pass. But this latest stuff, this shimmering and now this voice… She didn't know about those and he wouldn't tell her, she'd certainly think he was losing his mind. He would try to ignore them, concentrate on his work, and maybe they'd go away. "Don't think you'll escape from me," the voice had said. Well that's exactly what he would think. Exactly.

That night he had a dream about his editor, Don. "The Golden Wolf is too common," he said. "*Cry of the Golden Wolf* is exactly right."

"But don't you think it's too much like a horror novel?" Jeff replied, and then he fell back to sleep.

ROBBIE

ROBBIE LIVED ON THE edge of town on Hazel Street, where the concrete road stopped and the gravel road started. Beyond his large back yard, a half mile of forest stretched to the river; maple, oak, wild cherry, ash, spruce, hemlock, pine and other trees, many of them draped with vines. To the west of the house, where the gravel began, was a line of trees and a one lane road going down to a cabin. Past that, a path went to the river.

His father had built their house with a fireplace—a Russian fireplace that threw off lots of heat. He figured that when the power went off in the winter—which it sometimes did in this part of Maine—he and his family would still be warm, and aside from that, burning wood would drastically reduce the oil bill, since he got the wood for free. There were plenty of fallen trees in the forest and he cut some up and split them into cordwood, stacking it in a shed attached to the garage. Now that Robbie was eight, he had the job of keeping the fire going, which he loved.

One time when Robbie was four, he walked with his father down the dirt road to the cabin, built before Hazel Street had houses. *Long* before. Rumor said it had been a hunting lodge when the town still let people shoot deer.

"Nobody's there right now," his father said. "A guy named Ed something owns the place but only uses it now and then, mostly in the summer when he fishes in the river. I'm showing you this because I don't want you coming here by yourself. That path over there leads to the river and the river is a dangerous place. Listen, can you hear it?"

Robbie did hear it and said he would never come here alone, but once last summer he and his best friend, Brett Weston, saw a car go down the lane and decided to investigate. They hid in the trees not far from the cabin wondering who was there, and Robbie sniffed his fingers.

Brett had asked him about this sniffing once. "It just makes me feel better," Robbie said.

Brett tried it. "It doesn't make *me* feel better," he said, and Robbie just shrugged. He would never tell Brett about clutching his penis to make himself feel better, it was too embarrassing. And he always wondered when he did it, what girls did. He had seen Jimmy Baker's naked little sister once and she didn't have a penis. So what did they do to make themselves feel better? Just sniffed their fingers, he guessed, though he never saw any girls do that.

They were watching the door of the cabin when Robbie said, "Whoever is staying here is a stranger. My parents said to beware of strangers."

"Mine too," Brett said in almost a whisper. "Stranger danger. Don't worry though, he's not gonna see us." Then he said, "What worries me is fishers. I hope there's none around."

"What's fishers?" Robbie said.

"My dad said they live down here. They're a real mean animal that eats cats, so you gotta watch out for Tofu."

"She does run off sometimes but I don't think she'll come here alone."

"And there's Lyme ticks down here too. They make you real sick. My dad knows this woman who— Hey, look."

A gray-haired man came out of the cabin to dump something into a black container. Robbie and Brett were perfectly still, and in that stillness they heard the faint roar of the river. As soon as the man went inside again, they ran back up the lane. They wondered who he was—maybe Ed?—and what he was doing? But he could never ask their parents since going down there was forbidden.

Hazel Street held only three houses on its southern side and four on its northern side. All had been built in the last ten years and more would be built soon, people said.

Robbie's house had been built—largely by his father— before he was born eight years ago, and he'd never lived anywhere else. He'd always hoped to have a brother, but it hadn't happened, no matter how much he begged his mother for one. He didn't have any cousins either: Uncle Victor and Aunt Ruth had no children, Aunt Lillian had never married, and his mother was an only child.

Brett Weston had a younger sister, Cheryl, and Robbie didn't want any sisters; they were a pain. Brett lived at the other end of the street, north side. He was half an inch shorter than Robbie (who was small for a third grader), had a shiny yellowish crewcut and wore glasses. He had set up a bullseye target in his yard and practiced his archery all year round. He had actually lost arrows in the snow.

The school where Robbie and Brett and Cheryl went was only a few hundred yards away from Brett's house. After that there were lots of houses, a fire station and a reservoir. Two blocks up was Main Street, with a grocery store, gas station, hardware store, gift shop and Lonny's Sandwich Stop, which had popsicles and ice cream bars.

The Saturday following Grammy Hastings' funeral, Robbie told his mother he wanted to go to Brett's house to show him the cane.

"That cane stays right here," Carol said. "It's very valuable. Ugly, but valuable."

"But it wants to go out."

"Oh it does, does it?"

"Yes."

"So you've already given it a personality."

"What's personality?"

"What somebody thinks, how they act."

"Well, I didn't give it any of that, it's just how it is."

Imagination off the charts, Carol thought.

"Please, Mom?"

She sighed. "Okay, just this once. But don't hurt it, for heavens sakes. Just show it to him and come right back."

"Thanks Mom, I will.

The cane that Grammy gave him—she called it "The Golden

Wolf"—had a mahogany shaft and a wolf's head handle made of solid gold. She'd given it to him a couple of days before she died.

"As if she had known she was going to die," Tony had said to Carol. "She would never part with it otherwise. She let us kids touch it only once—just *once*—in all those years we lived with her, then put it away again. Which was fine with us, it looked *nasty*. We were scared of it. I'm *still* a little scared of it, those *fangs*. It sat in her library closet forever, then she suddenly gave it to Robbie. I thought I might get it, it's an antique, that gold head alone is worth a bunch, but no, she decided to give it to Rob—who isn't scared of it, I guess."

Grammy's Victorian stood in the oldest part of town among other Victorians, all of which had been built at the end of the previous century and, for the most part, had been kept up. Robbie liked to go over there and explore the house and neighborhood, so different from the modern neighborhood he lived in. He saw the rooms that his father and Uncle Victor and Aunt Lillian had occupied as children, all empty now, and wondered what it had been like to live with Grammy and her husband, whose name was Roger, back in the olden days.

One time, about a year ago, Grammy showed The Golden Wolf to Robbie in her library. "It comes from Romania," she said, "That's where my parents' family is from. In Romania people believe in spirits, spirits everywhere, it's not like here. This cane was made a long time ago by a wizard, a highly spiritual person."

"A wizard?"

"That's what my parents said."

"I know the Wizard of Oz."

"But he turned out to be a fake. This wizard was real."

"Like Harry Potter."

"Who?"

"He's this kid who went to wizard school. I saw some movies of it."

"Another nonsensical story," Grammy said. 'I'm talking about a *real* wizard. According to my grandparents he had a pet wolf, thus the cane's head. Now here's what I want you to do. Wind up the truck."

The ice truck had a motor in it. He wound it as Grammy told him to.

"Now hold it in your hand."

He did.

"Do you feel the vibrations?"

He said he did.

"Now put it down."

He did that too and the truck ran across the floor and into the wall. Then she handed the cane to him, telling him not to touch its golden head, and asked, "Do you feel vibrations from the cane?"

"I do," he said. "Just little ones, not like the truck."

"Good, good," Grammy said.

"Now tell me. Do you hear anything? A voice?"

He frowned. There *was* a voice, but he barely heard it—almost like one of his thoughts. "I do," he said.

"And what is it saying?"

There were words he didn't understand but then he heard *good boy* and told his Grammy that.

Her eyes went wide. "You are the one!" she said. "At last, the one who deserves possession! —Which none of my children did. There's a magical spirit in that cane and in time, as you grow, you will learn how to use it—you and you alone—and it will protect you and help you in many ways."

He told all this to Brett, who was messing around with a toy cop car on the sidewalk in front of his house. His dad was a cop; he helped people in trouble and also arrested them. He said, "The cane is magical? So how does it work?"

"I don't know yet."

"It looks mad, and its teeth look sharp."

"They are."

"It's really cool. Can I hold it?"

"Okay," Robbie said, "but watch out for those teeth." He handed it over.

Brett thrust it here and there.

"Do you feel anything?" Robbie asked. "Like a buzzing?"

"No."

"I guess I'm the only one who can feel it, but I didn't yet today."

"How old is it?"

"More than a hundred years, I guess. Maybe two hundred years, I don't really know. It's from Romania."

"Oh, I know where that is. There's vampires there."

"No kidding."

"Yeah, I saw this movie once."

"That's where my grandmother's parents were from a long time ago. She told me the cane has powers."

"Like what?"

"She told me that it can help me. Help protect me."

"From what? Like Buddy Lash?" Buddy was a real mean kid, two years older than they were, who lived a couple of blocks past the school.

"Maybe," Robbie said. "It can also be my guide."

"What do you mean? It can talk?"

"Maybe, I don't really know, but sometimes now I hear these voices in my dreams—like foreign words. And also regular words."

"And you think it's the cane?"

"I do. Grammy said I can never give it to anyone or sell it or bad things will happen. She said I will know when to pass it on and who to pass it to, I guess when I get old, like her. Here, give it back."

Brett did. "It's really cool. You could bring it to class and tell everybody about it."

"Oh no, I can't do that, my mom won't let me. She didn't even want me to bring it here."

"Oh. Well, you want to go down to the cabin and explore?"

"With the cane?"

"It might protect us."

"No, I have to take it home."

"Let's go to Lonny's then."

"First I have to take the cane back," Robbie said, "I promised my mom, and then we can go."

Brett suddenly looked alarmed. His eyes went wide and he said, "Gazorp!"

This was the favorite expression of Gordie the Gumshoe

Groundhog, their favorite cartoon character, who used it when he came across a clue or other surprise.

"What's up?" Robbie said, and then he saw. Buddy Lash was walking past the school, headed their way.

"No Rocky at least," said Brett. "I hate that dog."

"I don't want him to see this cane."

"Let's go inside."

In Brett's kitchen his mother, thin, with hair the straw-like color of her son's, said, "What a beautiful cane. Your grandmother gave it to you?"

"Yes."

"Rather sinister-looking, though."

"What's that mean?"

"Kinda scary. That wolf looks angry."

"I guess so," Robbie said. "It has sharp teeth."

They looked outside again and Buddy was nowhere in sight.

"I'm going home now," Robbie said. "My mother worries about the cane."

"I don't blame her," Brett's mother said. "That gold head must be worth a mint."

"I guess so," Robbie said.

When he walked back home, a large black bird overhead cried out. It seemed to be following him. Grip, he thought. A bird like Grip. Well maybe it was just a crow and not a raven, but it gave him chills.

JEFF

JEFF WOULD GET UP in the morning at various times, depending on when he had gone to bed. He'd put wood on the fire, make coffee, eat a slice of buttered toast, smoke a cigarette, then go to his desk.

He'd been working on his new project for several weeks; it was slowly, grudgingly coming along. Sometimes he thought that he didn't know where he was going with it, which wasn't unusual; he always expected to hit blank spots.

You know the drill. You try and try and try to remember the name of a person, place or plant to no avail. Then suddenly, out of the blue, it comes to you: "rose campion!" Well that was the same way it worked with his writing. Stuck, stuck, stuck, lying awake at night, then bingo! the path becomes clear—if he's lucky, which most of the time he was.

But sometimes the subconscious lightning took what seemed like forever. This was happening more and more frequently now; his progress was much more sluggish than usual. Old age? he thought. Already?

Most days he would work for a couple of hours then take a break, eat a snack, go back to his desk for another few hours, eat lunch, take a nap, take a walk to the river if the weather was good, read things related to what he was doing, look over his morning work, eat dinner, and then, if he still had juice, he'd head back to his desk again. If the juice had run out he'd go to bed early.

But once he started to write a book it was with him constantly, it never quit. Some writers thought about writing only when they were actually doing it, but he sure wasn't one of them. Once he got underway, half of his brain was in the real world and half in a fantasy world. And some of his best work was done late at night.

Today, however, he hadn't been good from the very start. He'd had what he thought was a great idea in a dream last night, but when he awoke he realized it was preposterous. How he hated it when that happened.

As he put more wood in the airtight stove, thoughts of the voice he had heard unnerved him. He went to his study, scanned what he'd done the day before, and just didn't feel the spark. He could force it, of course, but instead he went to the window and looked outside.

A fresh coating of snow had fallen overnight. So beautiful. But his thoughts were distant, dull.

Back home he had looked up visual migraines on his computer a number of times and learned that certain people heard growling sounds or whistling sounds, stuff like that, but almost never voices. Did voices mean…?

Hold on, he remembered now. He had heard occasional voices back when he was drinking heavily. He would run water into the sink and it seemed to be talking, saying things he didn't understand. When his jacket rubbed against his neck as he was driving, it sounded like words. Driving! In that condition! Now *that* was crazy. But *this* voice was more coherent, spoke in sentences. It had to be caused by the migraine, he was sure of it. But had all that drinking back then changed his brain somehow, and the changes were just showing up? Some people quit smoking for years, but then they got lung cancer later in life—because they had smoked when young.

He decided to take a break and eat some cereal. Instant oatmeal this time with some raisins thrown in. As he ate he thought about Sandra, her girls, the book he was writing, the worrisome voice again. He drank more coffee, smoked another cigarette. Got to cut down on these things, he thought. Or just quit. Easy enough to say, but he was addicted.

He had let the fire die to coals and started it up again. If Sandra was here she would never let the fire die, she was always colder than he was.

He went back to his work but thoughts of the voice kept interfering. Maybe a walk would clear his head. He put on his jacket and hat and boots and started out.

It took him ten minutes to reach the river. Its banks were rimmed with ice. He wondered how cold it would have to be to freeze all the way across. He had some commitments to keep in the city and hoped he'd be gone from here before it got that cold.

He headed back, his mind no clearer than when he had started out. Then he saw a small hole in his vision.

Again. Two days in a row. But that was to be expected. There would probably be a third day, a fourth, a fifth, a sixth—the "migrainous state"—then nothing for weeks. Don't consume any red wine, chocolate or sharp cheese, the doctors had warned. All things that he loved, of course. What kind of research had been done on that? It was totally useless advice. Today all he'd had was black coffee and instant oatmeal, and now...

By the time he reached the cabin the migraine was in its final stage, with large blind spots—scotomas the doctors called them—and yellow and green jagged lights. The edge of his vision was shimmering wildly. When he entered the kitchen a voice said, "Enjoy your walk?"

TONY

"SO NOW WHAT?" CAROL asked.

"I don't know," Tony said.

It was Friday. He'd come home early from work and she didn't smell any alcohol on his breath. "Four hours last night," he said. "I practically tore the place apart."

"It has to be there somewhere."

"I just thought it would be in her desk. Where else would she keep it? I'll go back tonight and give it another try."

"Victor is very upset."

"I know. But he's already well aware of what it says."

"You're sure it leaves everything to the church."

"Well, almost everything. Except the house—and all that's in it—which goes to Lillian."

"Who's ecstatic, of course."

"Of course."

"What do you think you could sell it for?"

"She'll never sell it."

"I realize that. But what do you think?"

"It needs work," Tony said. "Dad used to take care of things but after he died, Mother just let the place run down. It needs a roof, foundation work, and paint both inside and out. Until that's done it wouldn't sell for much."

Carol frowned. She thought for a minute then said, "What I can't understand is why she gave her cane to Robbie instead of to you, or even to Victor or Lillian."

"I can't understand it either. I was shocked. I actually thought she'd take it to her grave."

"Weird," Carol said. "Well listen, you really have to find that will. If only she'd used a lawyer." Carol worked as a part-time accountant for a local company, knew some lawyers, and tried a number of times to get Tony's mother to work with one, but she wouldn't listen.

"She never trusted lawyers," Tony said.

"If she'd used one, they'd have a copy of her will in their files, but now…When did she tell you where it was?"

"I don't know, a year ago maybe."

"A year ago. She didn't trust lawyers but she trusted you. Trusted you to remember."

Tony shrugged.

"Let me go with you this time."

"No," Tony said. "You don't have to do that."

"I want to go."

"I'll take Robbie," Tony said. "Maybe she told him where it was."

"Why would she ever do that?"

"Who knew what she would ever do? I mean she gave him the *cane*."

"So when do you plan to go?"

"Right now."

———— ◊ ————

Robbie was out back beside the garage, fooling around with the cane. Carol didn't want him out there with it, thought he should keep it in his room, but Tony said, "Hey, Mother gave it to him, if he wants to play with it…"

"I'd hate to see him break it," Carol said. "Or lose it."

"Don't worry," Tony said with a little laugh.

Grammy had taken possession of the cane when her mother died. She was twenty years old at the time. As she handed it over to Robbie right before her own death she said, "The Wolf belongs to you now. Whenever you are in trouble, hold it tight, and it will help. It's helped me many times."

Robbie was puzzled by this; he didn't know what she meant. But it did feel good to hold the cane, made him feel stronger than usual. And when he squeezed it hard, he pictured Grammy and thought he could hear her voice—or somebody else's voice—far, far away.

Carol called him inside. He left the cane in the mudroom and entered the kitchen. She told him the plan: he and his father were going to Grammy's house to look for the missing will. Grammy had never talked to him about it, had she? No, never, he said.

"Too bad," she said, then added, "I don't want you to take the cane."

"Why not?"

"I just don't want you to. You might leave it there."

"Dad won't let me forget it. And it might help us find the will."

"I doubt that very much."

"But Grammy said—"

"I don't care what Grammy said, I don't want you to take

the cane." She was sure it was worth big bucks, and maybe she could talk Tony into selling the stupid thing once Robbie tired of it.

"Sometimes when I hold it I hear voices."

Carol rolled her eyes. *Imagination.* "Oh really?" she said. "What kind of voices?"

"Sometimes Grammy's, sometimes different ones. Some of them are foreign ones I think."

"Uh-huh."

"They're far away."

"I see."

"You don't believe me but it's true."

"I believe you."

Robbie frowned. "If you won't let me take the cane, can I take Tofu?"

"No, she might run off. If she ran off at Grammy's you might never find her."

"I'll keep an eye on her."

"She stays right here."

"Oh, Mom."

Tony put the key in the ornate front door lock and turned and the door came open.

And there was that smell: of age and mustiness that Robbie always linked to Grammy. He went through the vestibule with his father and into the dingy high-ceilinged parlor with its brown velvet drapes and thick Victorian carpet.

They walked past Grammy's leather armchair. It was

strange to not see her sitting in it. She had always been there whenever they came, with a box of coins and butterscotch candies wrapped in yellow cellophane on her lap. She would always offer one candy to Robbie, just one. "More than that and you could get cavities," she'd always said.

Next to the chair was the stand that held Grip, her raven, empty now. It was a nasty bird, it had bitten his thumb, and he hated it. Grammy had never let it loose while he was here, and he was glad that it was dead. But Grammy had loved it. "It's my watch bird," she said. "When somebody comes to the door it shrieks like mad."

Tony looked here and there all over again, stewing about the will. Why Lillian would want this old decrepit hulk—that she and he and Victor had grown up in—instead of her new apartment, was a mystery. But she and his mother had a special bond with the wacko church they attended, and maybe that was the reason. Maybe Lil would renovate the place, restore it to the way it had been when they were kids, but probably not. She probably liked it rundown, just the way it was.

Tony went through all the drawers again, which were filled with stuff, and Robbie helped. It made him feel creepy to look at Grammy's clothes and sheets and towels and all the rest and he sniffed his fingers. He picked up the soldier figurine from the library shelf. He really wanted it, but the figurine and the rest of the stuff in the house belonged to Aunt Lillian now. He wished he had brought Grammy's cane, The Golden Wolf; he knew it would help him find the missing will, tell him where to look.

The massive rolltop desk in the parlor was filled with

pencils, pens, erasers, scissors, tape, and tons of papers which Tony looked through hurriedly, as he'd seen them all the night before. Nothing important there as far as he could tell.

"Well, let's go, Rob," he said. "I'm hungry for dinner, how about you?"

"Me too. But you didn't find it."

"No."

"What happened to that box that Grammy used to have? The one with the coins and butterscotch?"

"A very good question," Tony said. "A very good question indeed."

At home, in the dining room, Tony took out his phone and called Victor.

"You still didn't find it? Do I have to go there myself?"

"Maybe you'll have better luck than me."

"But you are the one she told about it."

"I know, but I just can't remember."

"You were drunk when she told you."

"I don't remember."

"You always fortified yourself before going over there—unless you were going there to fix something."

"I can't deny it."

"What the hell were you so afraid of? We grew *up* in that house."

"I don't know, Vic. I don't know."

"We really need that will to wrap things up."

"You already know what it says."

"We need it!"

"Okay, okay, I'll give it another shot when I get the chance."

When he got off the phone, Carol, putting the meal on the dining room table, said, "I can't believe you still haven't found it."

"You'd think she'd put it in an obvious place—or told us about it on her deathbed."

"She was always so perverse."

"She was that, all right."

Robbie sat at the table, starving. Tony went into the kitchen and got a beer, came back, sat down. "Okay, let's eat," he said, and Robbie thought: The Wolf knows where to find the will. I know it does!

JEFF

STILL IN THE KITCHEN, fighting the migraine light show in his eyes, he saw the man in the living room, a silhouette. *Not again*, he thought. *Ignore it!*

"But you can't," said the voice.

It had read his mind! —Which proved this whole business was *in* his mind. Nothing could be done about these auras the doctors said, there was no sense resisting them. But damn! he thought. I come to this cabin in the woods to get away from distractions only to find this guy, who is ruining everything. Was it self-destruction? Is that what it was? He didn't know.

He'd read that if you had tinnitus—noise in the ears—instead of trying to ignore it, focusing on it could tone it down. So why not focus on this apparition, what did he have to lose? Feeling totally foolish he said, "Who are you?" expecting to get no reply, but the man said, "I told you before. A friend."

Jeff's stomach cramped. So this was the way it was going to end, like something in one of his books? He'd imagined this countless times—as well as countless other ways to die.

One of those ways would at last come true—or one that he hadn't thought of yet. But please, not this one, not insanity.

He was starting to tremble now, and realized he hadn't felt quite this bad since before he quit drinking.

He stepped into the living room, thinking, Okay, calm down, just focus on it, go along with it. Breaking into a sweat he said, "What's your name?"

"I'm waiting for you to give me one," the man said.

Oh, you are, Jeff thought. "All right then, I'll call you…Tony."

"That name is already in play. Choose another one."

My god, Jeff thought, *he even knows what I'm writing.* Then he thought, *Well of course he does!* "Okay," he said, "not Tony, Richard." He'd never named a character that in any book of his—as far as he could remember.

"That's fine, let's go with it."

"Okay, Richard it is. Now what do you want?"

"I want to talk. You aren't working well today and I want to know why."

Now this really ticked Jeff off. "I come to this place for peace and quiet and what do I get? I get *you!*"

"And who is to blame for that?"

"Me? You're saying that *I'm* to blame?"

"Could be."

"Am I to blame for my migraines? I've tried everything I can to stop them and nothing works."

"You're not responsible for the migraines, but the way they manifest themselves…"

"Is my responsibility?" Jeff said. "Is that what you're saying?" He was suddenly seized by an anger so strong that it drowned his fear. "Get out of here!" he said. "Get out! Right now!"

"I can't, not yet," Richard said, "I'm compelled to talk," and he took a step forward.

His face was in shadow, but visible now, and Jeff didn't recognize it. The man simply stood there, his hands at his sides. He was just about six feet tall, of average build, and about Jeff's age, his brown hair parted on the left, a blue dress shirt, a tie. He did not look angry or threatening. "I have waited a long time, you know," he said, and his mild tone seemed genuine, not a mask for madness or rage.

"No," Jeff said, "I don't know," and his heart was racing. "I don't know who you are, or what you're doing here, I just want you to leave."

"I won't stay long," Richard said. "Not this time. But I have a few things to say before I go."

"Say them then," Jeff said.

Richard smiled. "How long do you think you have?"

Jeff was totally tense and alert. His heart was loud as he said, "What the hell are you talking about?"

"How many chances do you think you'll get? You're fifty-nine. Time's running out."

Jeff told himself: *Calm, calm.* "Running out on what?" he said. "Chances at what?"

Richard stood motionless, hands at his sides. His right arm was brighter than his left and his right ear was glowing yellow. "Chances to do your true work," he said.

Jeff took a deep breath. His temples were starting to throb and his mouth was sour. "You've come here to tell me about my true work?" he said.

"Exactly."

Jeff sniffed. "Well then tell me," he said. "What is it? Engineer? Carpenter? Brain surgeon? Five-star chef?"

"You know what your true work is," said Richard.

"Well how about a little hint," Jeff said with all the sarcasm he could muster.

"Let's start with this," Richard said. "Do I look familiar to you?"

"No. Not at all."

"Not in the slightest?"

"No."

"I'm surprised," Richard said. "You knew me quite well once."

Jeff's mind was churning. He thought that maybe he *did* know this guy. But know him well? That was another story, no, he'd never known him well. He had never known hardly *anyone* well, and certainly not *this* guy."

"Another story," Richard said. "That's it, what I've come to see you about, another story."

In sudden bewilderment, Jeff said, "What?" *Another story.* He had *thought* that, not said it aloud. But that was further confirmation that all this—"

"You should be writing another story," Richard said.

"Oh?" Jeff said, his confusion tinged with a fresh jolt of fear. "And what other story is that?"

"Perhaps my story."

So *that's* what this is all about, Jeff thought. Good God, another one of *those.* But this one is serious, this one is heavy duty. All writers ran into these people, it came with the territory. "I have an absolutely marvelous story for you, you simply have to write it." How many times had he heard that line? And how many times had that marvelous story turned out to be the story of the speaker's life?

"I have too many projects as it is," Jeff said to the man, who continued to stand at the edge of the halo of light. It was his standard response. He never said, "Your story is absolutely boring and banal to anyone but yourself." Or: "It is indeed a marvelous concept—but not for me."

People who didn't write couldn't fathom that. If they gave you an idea, they felt that you ought to be grateful and run with it. They couldn't seem to understand there was no way in hell you could execute what they told you. On the contrary, they seemed to think that all a writer had to do was pull the proper lever—romance, detective, thriller, whatever—and a book would come pouring out.

"On the other hand, it might be *your* story," Richard said. "About what you're going through now."

"Oh great," Jeff said. "Another story about a writer. People just can't wait to read about that."

"Your current projects are not essential," Richard said.

The arrogance of the guy! "Not essential to you," Jeff said, "but highly essential to me. They allow me to *live*."

"They're killing you."

His bland tone riled Jeff. *But remember*, he told himself, *it's all in your mind.* Your *disordered* mind. "You know about my projects," he said.

"I do," Richard said. "The one you're working on now, where will it get you? What's the point of this young adult stuff?"

So angry now his arms were shaking, Jeff said, "Young adult? You think what I'm working on is YA?"

"I do. No foul language, no sex scenes. I think you're betraying your talent."

Jeff sniffed sarcastically. "Oh, you do. Do you think *Treasure Island* was YA? Or *Kidnapped*? What about *Tom Sawyer* or *Huckleberry Finn*, *Oliver Twist*, *The Catcher in the Rye*?"

"They could all be considered YA these days," Richard said.

"Oh, right. Do you know that Borges loved Robert Louis Stevenson? *Borges*? As complex a writer as that?"

"Hard to figure, but maybe he was a child at heart. And maybe you are too. But I think it's time to find out."

"Oh, do you? *Do* you? Let me tell you something. Half of the people who read YA books are adults, so if the book I'm writing *is* YA, what have I got to lose?"

At this, Richard simply smiled. He said, "I'm fading now and have to go. Thanks for giving me a name." Then he raised his right hand, which was throwing off golden sparks, took one step backward, and was gone.

Gone. He didn't walk out of the room, he was simply *gone*.

The migraine had died out now except for some grainy stuff at the edges of Jeff's vision—and a mild headache. *How am I supposed to work after that?* he asked himself. His heart was still beating fast but he wasn't shaking anymore.

"YA," he said out loud. "Is that what people will think?" He took a deep breath, exhaled, then put more wood on the fire.

The full-length mirror hung on the wall to the left of the airtight stove. Jeff caught his reflection in it and thought: It's true what Richard said, time's running out. Crow's feet at my eyes, gray hair, diminished energy… He's right about that.

This point had been brought home forcefully by a recent incident. Jeff had run into a former AA member on the street, Bill Hall, they talked about the merits of continuing the program, then Bill said, "Hey, you're a writer, so here's some interesting news for you. My son Sam, who's twenty-six, just had a novel accepted by Wallace & Bell."

Jeff felt a sudden shock. For a moment he felt a bit faint, but quickly recovered. "That's wonderful," he said. "That's a really good company, maybe the best."

"That's what Sammy tells me." Bill said. "They told him they really love the book and they're going to promote the devil out if it. It's getting an ad in two consecutive *New Yorker*s, and also a brief review."

"That's fabulous," Jeff said. "I'd love to read it when it's available."

"I have your email address and I'll send you a notice."

"Great."

"So what are you up to? Any new books?"

"I'm working on one," Jeff said, and he felt a twinge in his heart. Wallace & Bell had turned down one of his books—the one he considered his best!

"Well, good luck with it," Bill said. "I gotta run, great seeing you again."

He went on his way and Jeff thought: Twenty-six! Wallace & Bell! The *son* of someone my age! Time *is* running out!

He lit a cigarette and went to the window, gazed at the peaceful snow-covered scene and thought: Twenty-six. That's how old I was when my failed first novel came out. But I didn't get published by Wallace & Bell. Comparing my publisher in those days with Wallace & Bell would be like comparing the local infirmary to the Mayo Clinic. You get published by Wallace & Bell and people take notice, you're seen in a different light, especially by reviewers. He frowned at the tip of the cigarette in his hand. I still can't understand why they didn't accept...

Then: Maybe I'm just not good enough, he thought. No, no, that can't be it, it must be...I'm a little bit out of step with the times. Much contemporary writing, poetry especially, valued the inscrutable, words detached from their meanings, and left him scratching his head. That has to be what people want, though. At least editors do.

Richard's words came back to him and he said aloud, "You *talked* to him. You actually talked to an apparition, had a *conversation* with him. With *yourself.* Now is that kind of crazy, or what? But maybe that's the last of 'Richard'—at least for a while."

He smoked. Or maybe not, he thought. I still have some migraine days ahead of me and if he returns...I guess I should see somebody. But who? And when?

ROBBIE

ON SATURDAY HE ROSE early, ate a quick breakfast and told his mother he was going to Brett's (which was a lie).

"You be back for lunch," Carol said.

"I will."

"You're not taking the cane are you?"

"Yeah, Brett wants to see it again."

"He should see it right here."

"I won't hurt it."

"Things happen," his mother said.

When no one was looking, Robbie took the key to Grammy's house from the mudroom hook and went outside. He put Tofu into the basket on his bike—without asking his mother—and put the cane across the handlebars. "We're going for a little ride and don't you jump out, Tofu." He didn't want to be in that old creepy house alone, and Tofu was good company.

It took less than ten minutes to get there. Robbie leaned his bike against the porch and went up the steps, Tofu trailing behind. He inserted the key in the lock and turned it and nothing happened. He tried it two more times and it worked and he went inside.

He was holding the cane, and squeezed it. Grammy had said to do this if he felt upset or worried and it would make him feel better. And it did.

That musty smell again and thoughts of Grammy, bright and confusing. A quick twinge of fear and he didn't know why. Then a sudden feeling he knew where to find the will.

He passed the empty bird stand where nasty Grip had perched. When it bit his thumb Grammy cried, "Grip!" and the bird said, "Murder!" It could talk, and this was one of the words it said.

Robbie went to the hallway and climbed the stairs to the library, Tofu at his heels. How many times had he been here, surrounded by all of Grammy's stuff, listening to her stories, looking at the photo album that went way back to Romania. The cane was in some of those ancient pictures! It must stay in the family, she'd told him. By "family" he thought she meant Aunt Lillian or Uncle Victor or his father, but then right before she died she gave it to *him*. "It is yours now," she said. "You will guard it and learn how to use it."

She had told him about the things on the shelves in the library: the cups, the steins, the stones, the shells, the little figurines. He had played with some of those figurines—and the ice truck, which he really loved—and hoped she would give them to him but she never had. Now Aunt Lillian owned them. Would she keep them? Or let him have them.

Feeling anxious now in the deathly quiet, he held the cane tight and soon felt a mild buzzing. His thoughts were a waterfall of disconnected words, but through all that confusion he heard a far-off voice urging him forward. Some of the words stood out: "Book," he heard, and the name

"Will Hamilton." The author of a book? He searched the bookshelves underneath the shelf of curios, and suddenly there it was: *Will Hamilton*. Not the author, but the title. The author was someone named Gerald Finch.

He reached out and took the book down. When he opened it, to his great surprise, it was hollow—and held the will!

"I found it!" He said aloud. "Tofu, I found it, Will Hamilton held…the will!"

But where was Tofu?

He called the cat and looked all around.

"We can go home now," he said. "Come on, Tofu."

She wasn't behind or under a chair, she wasn't in the hall. Downstairs?

With the cane and the will, he went down. "Tofu!" he called. His voice was muffled by the drapes and rug and ornate furniture. He wanted to get *out* of here. "Tofu! We're going home!"

He thought of what his mother had said: *If Tofu ran off at Grammy's, you might never find her.* Oh why had he brought her, why hadn't he listened—

Then Tofu appeared out of nowhere, startling him. She was suddenly just *there*—and looked a bit scruffy. "Where in the world did you get to?" Robbie said. "You shouldn't run off like that. Okay," he said, and opened the heavy front door again and went outside.

He locked the door, put Tofu in the basket on his bike and, holding the cane and the will, headed home.

His father was not around and his mother was in her sewing

room. He went to his father's desk and put the will in the shallow drawer below the desktop. "There," he said to Tofu.

And sure enough, when his father came home, he opened that drawer and found the will. "Carol, I got it," he said at the door to her sewing room. "It was there in my desk all the time."

"How could you possibly overlook it?" she said.

"It was there with a bunch of other papers. You know I'm not the neatest guy in the world."

"Have you looked at it?"

"I have."

"Does it say what we thought it would?"

"It does. Lil gets the house and its contents, Vic gets the old stamp album, the stocks and bonds go to the church. The only thing we get is the box of coins, which are surely worth something. But we can't find it."

"Maybe it's in your desk—under all the papers."

"Very funny," Tony said.

"I think Victor took it," Carol said.

"Come on."

"He went to the house before you did and took stuff that belonged to him."

"But he wouldn't take *my* stuff."

"You better get in touch with him and give him the bad news. Which he already knows."

"Damn!" Victor said into the phone. "I guess I should have been a religious nut like Lillian."

"You would have sold the place."

"Damn right!"

"And Lillian will never let it go, she loved Mother so much. What do you think her stocks and bonds were worth?"

"Plenty," Victor said, and Tony thought, It just wasn't fair what his mother had done. He ran errands for her, did odd jobs around the place, it just wasn't right to give everything to that church. "By the way," he said. "That box of coins she used to have on her lap. She left them to me, but they seem to have disappeared. You haven't seen them, have you?"

"Of course not," Victor said.

Robbie played with his truck on the living room rug and heard all this and started to feel what he'd felt at Grammy's house. Anxiety. Fear. He sniffed his fingers.

When Tony hung up the phone, Robbie went to the cane for comfort and squeezed it tight. He felt a buzz and his thoughts took a sudden twist. "*Victor*," they said.

LILLIAN

THE FOLLOWING MORNING, AUNT Lillian picked him up in her old four-door Chevy. She rambled on about what a wonderful person Grammy had been while Robbie was lost in thoughts of his own—mixed in with other thoughts that were *not* his own.

At the church, they sat up front in the pew they always sat in. Lillian said hello to the woman he'd seen at the funeral, the one with the golden earrings. "Mrs. Carney can see the future," Lillian said and Robbie thought: That's impossible, nobody knows what the future holds.

All of the congregation believed what the pastor preached: That the spirit survived the change called death. The world was full of spirits and they were everywhere, among them right this minute.

Last year, when he was in second grade, a girl he didn't like very much named Andrea Fisk had died of the flu. Was her spirit here? It was creepy to think so. Was she looking down at him? Would her spirit last forever? Did Aunt Lillian know the answers to these questions?

She bent down close to him now and whispered,

"Grammy's spirit is with us, can you feel it?"

"Yes," Robbie said, but it was a lie.

After the service, they went to the cemetery. Robbie didn't want to go, but Lillian insisted. In the car he said, "Aunt Lillian, what makes flowers and vegetables grow?"

"Why spirits, of course," she said.

As she prayed by her dead mother's grave, Robbie wandered among the stones. All these people were dead, and someday he too would be dead. But their spirits? He heard a rasping croak then and looked up.

A black bird sat on the branch of a leafless tree. It croaked again, and Robbie felt a cramp in his stomach, then felt a vibration run all through his body, felt words flowing through him, words he couldn't understand. They were not really thoughts but underneath his thoughts like the buzzing of bees in a hive. They were pushing at him, wanting him to do things, but what? Were they the spirits of the dead surrounding him? He felt on the verge of an asthma attack.

He hurried back to Aunt Lillian and said, "I want to go home. I want to go home right now!"

"I must finish my prayers first," she said. "You must learn to have patience, Robbie."

"No! Right now!"

In the car he said, "I saw Grip."

"Oh Robbie, please. You know as well as I do that Grip is dead."

"But I saw him. I saw him a couple of days ago too."

"I was some other bird," Aunt Lillian said.

"No, Grip! It was Grip!"

"Such foolishness," Aunt Lillian said.

ROBBIE

ROBBIE USED HIS BREATHERS when he got home and warded off an attack. And later that afternoon he went with his parents to Victor and Ruth's house for dinner. Lillian had been invited but she declined.

Victor asked Robbie to bring the cane as he'd never really been given a good chance to see it, and Tony gave permission.

"It really does look fierce," Ruth said, and Victor said, "It goes way back, *way* back, how far I guess we'll never know. Fierce but beautiful in a weird kind of way. Did Mother ever tell you it had powers?"

"She did," Tony said. He had already drunk three beers, and Carol glared at him to keep him from drinking a fourth.

"What rot," Victor said. "But she believed it. She kept it in her library closet most of the time, but other times she held it on her lap—and sometimes *talked* to it! Whenever the library door was shut, that's what she was doing. I know because I made a mistake and opened that door once, thinking that she was downstairs, and there she was squeezing the Wolf on her lap with her eyes closed. She opened them up right quick and angrily told me to scram."

"You never told me that before," Tony said.

"Oh yeah, she was really ripped. I always thought that maybe I or maybe you…Lillian didn't want it of course, it frightened her, and who ends up getting it? Robbie."

"She swore that it helped her," Tony said. "And maybe it did, things always seemed to work out in her favor."

"You're right," Victor said. "The day after I surprised her in the library, a woman she hated had a heart attack. But to blame that on the cane…ridiculous."

They told more stories about their mother, some of the outlandish things she did, then Tony took Victor aside and asked for a loan.

"Again?" Victor said.

"Not a lot," Tony said. "Just enough to get me through this small rough patch."

"You're always having rough patches," Victor said. "And may I remind you that you haven't paid off the last loan I gave you?"

Hearing this made Robbie's stomach tighten. While no one was looking he sniffed his fingers then went to the entryway, where he'd put the cane, and picked it up.

He squeezed it; as soon as he did, he felt stronger. A buzzing and sudden voice over the usual constant run of words in his head urged him to go upstairs.

It guided him to Victor's study, guided him to open the bottom drawer of the desk. When he did, he was shocked. Ga*zorp*! The box of coins!

There was still some butterscotch left and he ate a piece to make himself feel better. Now what? Then suddenly he heard the voice. It said to take the box downstairs.

He did, and placed it on the parlor rug. The adults were still in the dining room. He knew his father wanted to smoke but Aunt Ruth would not allow it.

He examined the coins. He had never seen them up close before. Some were from other countries but most were from America, and they were old—from before 1820—and a lot of them were gold.

His father and Uncle Victor came in from the dining room and Victor was frowning, probably still upset from talk about money. He suddenly stopped. And Tony said, "What in the world? Where did that come from, Robbie?"

"Upstairs," Robbie said.

Tony turned to his brother. "So you took it."

"Never!" Victor said. "I have no idea how it got here."

"I'll bet."

"I swear."

"It belongs to me," Tony said.

Victor looked flustered. "Yes," he said, "it does."

Tony bent over and picked it up. "I can't believe it, you actually stole it."

"I did not!"

"It wouldn't be here if you didn't."

"I got Jerry to help me move some stuff out of Mother's right after she died and he must have taken it and put it here."

"Oh, right," Tony said. He held the box under his arm and said, "We'll be going now. A very unpleasant end to an unpleasant afternoon."

"We'll discuss this later," Victor said. As he walked to the door he said, "You realize Mother gave me almost nothing, just those stamps, which aren't worth nearly as much as those coins."

"You don't need anything," Tony said. He tapped the box. "Thanks for the loan."

"He stole it," Carol said as they drove back home. "He knew it belonged to you and he stole it."

Robbie, in the car's back seat, felt worse than ever. His stomach was tight and he sniffed his fingers. The cane was sending streams of words through his head: *box coins stairs Grip Will Hamilton…* He put the cane down on the floor and the words receded.

"You're right," Tony said. "He has a key to the house and the box was just sitting there, so…"

"Some brother you have."

"Well maybe he didn't know it was mine. At the time he went to the house he hadn't seen the will."

"He knew, all right."

Don't argue, Robbie thought. *Please don't.*

"Whatever," his father said. "I have it now."

"Those people," Carol said. "At least you didn't drink too much."

"No, Carol, I was a good boy tonight."

JEFF

"WHAT I'M SAYING IS, I think you should take your work to another level. Something not so ordinary."

The migraine had come at night again. He had gone to the kitchen for apple juice when it began then put a few sticks of wood on the fire and sat on the couch to wait it out, hoping that "Richard" was gone for good. But as soon as the jagged lights began to fade, there he was again. Black shirt this time, no tie. And his face and his hands were glowing.

"Another level," Jeff said to himself. Or *was* it to himself?

"You're better than the work you're engaged in now."

"And what would you like me to do?" Jeff said. "Address the world's problems? Teach people how to live? Oh sure, I'm an expert at that."

Richard laughed. "No, no, just something a bit more …elevated. I don't mean you can reach the *Ulysses* heights or anything like that, but few people do."

"*Ulysses!* That disjointed mess! Obscure sentence fragments, Latin phrases, nonsensical rhymes… Joyce wrote it to puzzle professors, and boy did he ever succeed. They're *still* puzzled. He did that stuff to prove he was superior. I have no interest in doing that."

"You're interested in pleasing the masses—*ordinary* people."

"Absolutely. Who wants to be mystified by a work of fiction? They want a *story*."

"True, in most cases. But what do *you* want?"

"I want to write a compelling story that has some substance to it."

"Do you think you're doing it?"

"I hope so. You probably know what I'm going to say, how couldn't you? A long time ago, when I was starting out and full of myself, I wrote a so-called "experimental" novel—my very first book! I heard of a start-up publisher through a friend, gave them a try, and they accepted it. It got panned by *Publishers Weekly*, bad reviews in the periodicals and sold five hundred and fourteen copies. Do you think I should try that again?"

"Maybe so. You're older now, your writing is more mature."

"*That* book was 'mature.' Most people, including reviewers, can't deal with anything different, and my book was different. I thought it was good, damn good, but few people understood it."

"You'll have to admit it was very strange. You wouldn't write something like that today."

"You're absolutely right. You see, I'm comfortable with what I'm doing now. The ordinary, as you said."

"However, your last book was rather...stale."

"I hate to agree, but I guess that's how Sandra felt about it too. I know she didn't like it much."

"I think what she told you is right on the nose. You need to step out of your comfort zone to fulfill yourself."

"You don't think I'm doing that?"

"Not in the way you really want to."

"Oh, so I should shake everything up? At this age? When I'm slowing down? When the plots take a long time taking shape? It's hard enough to write the stuff I'm writing now, to make all those daily decisions, let alone go off in a different direction. To me, doing the same kind of thing gets harder and harder. I struggle with every book. With every sentence."

"I suggest that you put all that effort to another use."

"Oh, do you? *Do* you? And who are you to lecture me? Who—"

"What about that book you started years ago? The one about the poet."

"You *would* have to bring that up."

"There was a lot of good in it."

"It got to a point where it didn't move forward. I gave it some time but it didn't budge."

"And then you abandoned it."

"You could say that, yes."

"I think you should look at it again."

"Well thanks for the advice."

Richard smiled and said, "Don't mention it."

Jeff frowned. "That shirt you're wearing," he said. "I had one exactly like that years ago."

"What a coincidence," Richard said, and then, still smiling, his face and hands began to glow brightly, blindingly, and he disappeared.

Jeff sighed and leaned back on the couch. The nerve of the guy!

But he had to admit there was truth in what he said. He *did* want to do something better than what he was working on—and something that Sandra would like. That's what he was *doing* here, for godsake. But he wasn't sure where he was going with what he was into now. He'd convinced himself that the time for doing something different had passed, that all he wanted to do these days was make this book as good as he possibly could. Or *was* that really all he wanted?

As he sat there smoking, staring at the airtight stove, he started to think of the mainstream novel Richard had mentioned. He still felt the concept was marvelous, full of complexity, color and depth—but he just could never get it past the sticking point. Maybe Richard was right, he *was* more mature, and maybe he should revisit it. These damn visions, why were they stirring things up?

The airtight was throwing off plenty of heat and he turned it down as he wondered: How long would he have to put up with this Richard crap? Forever? He would have to put up with the migraines forever, so maybe so. He'd ignored the apparition and that hadn't worked. He'd engaged it—had even *named* it— which hadn't worked either. All he could do was wait, and oh, how he hated to wait.

TONY

TONY MANAGED TO SELL the coins for a very good sum to a dealer he'd dealt with before. He paid off the rest of what he owed Victor, and also a gambling debt that Carol didn't know about. There was still some money left, so he put a down payment on a new car.

"Why?" Carol said.

"Mine is on its last legs. It has a hundred and fifty thousand miles on it."

"It runs perfectly fine. And no rust."

"It's only a matter of time," Tony said. "It could die at any minute."

"Why did you have to get such an *expensive* one?"

"It will last forever."

"And what about *my* car? It has more miles than yours."

"But you never go anywhere. I travel all over the place to look at properties, where do *you* go? No more than fifteen miles away. I need a new, reliable car."

"Oh Tony, I don't know what to do with you, I really don't."

"Everything will be fine, Carol, wait and see."

Overhearing this conversation, Robbie thought he might

have an asthma attack. He went to the cane and squeezed it tight and felt instantly better. He suddenly realized his father was right to buy the car. He *did* need it for his work. And whose money was it, anyway? Grammy had given the coins to his father, not to his mother. *That's right,* he heard something say in his head. A voice, or just a thought?

"He's giving me a hard time again," Tony said.

"Over what?" Carol said. "Your quota?"

"Yeah."

"It's the third month in a row."

"Well how can I help it if people aren't buying? I'm doing the best I can."

"I wonder."

"What's *that* supposed to mean?"

"It means you get discouraged and give up and spend your afternoons at the Rusty Bucket. How many times have I smelled alcohol on your breath when you come home?"

"Not many."

"Plenty."

"Once or twice," Tony said. He was quiet a minute then said, "Okay, but it's just so depressing to put so much effort into a thing and have it amount to nothing."

"You should find another job."

"Doing what? All I know is sales."

"You have transferable skills."

"Oh sure."

"We've been through this so many times before, Tony, so many times. One thing you really *must* do is stop gambling."

"Easier said than done."

"It's just so *crazy*."

Tony shook his head. "Just one big hit would do it," he said. "Just one."

"How many dreamers say that? Again and again and again."

"But somebody always wins."

Carol simply sighed.

ROBBIE

ROBBIE LISTENED TO THIS. His chest tightened up and he held his cane. And the rush of thoughts arose again: *house desk book go back go back go back*...so insistent he knew that he had to do it. But not alone this time and not with Tofu.

He went to Brett's and found him shooting arrows at his target behind the house. "Bullseye!" Brett said.

"You're really getting good," Robbie said.

"You want to take a turn?"

"Some other time. Right now I'm going to my dead grandmother's house, you want to come?"

"Yeah, that sounds really cool."

Brett told his mother he was going bike riding with Robbie and off they went.

On his grammy's porch Robbie twisted the key in the lock—just once—and went inside. "This place is really spooky," Brett said.

As they crossed the parlor floor Robbie said, "This is the stand where Grip the raven sat. He could talk."

"No kidding."

"Yeah, he didn't say too many words, but he could talk. One of the words he said was 'murder.'"

"Ga*zorp*! Where is he now?"

"They say he's dead. That he died the same day my grandmother did. But I wonder. I saw him in the coffin with her but maybe he was just faking."

"I saw a black bird like that around my house the other day."

"And I saw one at the cemetery."

"What were you doing *there*?"

"My aunt made me go with her after church."

"I don't go to church."

"You're lucky," Robbie said. "My aunt believes in spirits, same as my grandmother did, that everything has one in them. Maybe I believe that too. Maybe the spirit of Grip passed into another raven, that's how it works."

"Well wouldn't the other raven already *have* a spirit?" Brett asked.

Robbie frowned. "I guess so, yes."

"So how could it have another one?"

"I don't really know. I never really thought about that."

"Did you ever read *A Christmas Carol*?"

"No, what's that?"

"It's about this mean old guy named Scrooge who has these spirits visit him at Christmas time. He learns these lessons from them, like how to be nice."

"Cool," Robbie said.

"It's just a story," Brett said. "I don't believe in spirits."

"My parents don't either, and I don't know what I believe, but it sure is weird about that bird."

He walked across the rug to the ornate desk and showed Brett how the rolltop worked.

"Cool," Brett said.

Robbie was quiet a minute then said, "Did you hear anything?"

"Like what?"

"Like footsteps, upstairs."

"No, I didn't."

"Listen."

"I don't hear anything."

They were quiet, then Robbie said, "I thought I heard something but maybe I didn't. But I don't want to go upstairs."

He suddenly saw that his hand was on the pull of the desk's bottom right side drawer. He didn't remember putting it there, but now, without thinking, he opened the drawer.

It was filled with papers and he rummaged through them. Had his father done the same thing? Or Uncle Victor? Surely they had, so there could be nothing important here. But the voice in his head said, *reach way back*. He did, and found an old brown envelope. Expecting nothing, he looked inside.

And saw three bankbooks. When he opened the first one his eyes went wide. "Ga*zorp*!" he said.

"What is it?" Brett said.

"This bankbook is for my father. And there's a lot of money in it. A lot!"

"Ga*zorp*!" Brett said. "So that's why you came here?"

"I don't know why I came here, but this is great! There's bankbooks for my aunt and uncle too! I'll leave the envelope here and they'll find it another time, but I'll take my father's now."

He suddenly heard those footsteps overhead. "Do you hear them?" he whispered to Brett.

Brett listened. "Maybe. Yes!"

"We have to get out of here!" Robbie said. "Let's go!"

He locked the front door and ran down the steps of the porch and the two of them jumped on their bikes. When Robbie looked back at the house he was sure that he saw a face at an upstairs window. I'll never come here again, he thought. Never!

At home he put the bankbook in the drawer where he'd put the will.

TONY

TONY FOUND IT AFTER dinner.

"Carol, you won't believe this," he said as he showed it to her.

"My god," she said. "It's wonderful! But I can't understand why you didn't see it before."

"I can't understand it either. My drawers are a total mess, but you'd think... Well, who cares, here it is."

"You'll be able to pay off a lot of your car loan."

"All of it!" He shook his head. "I remember when I was very young my mother telling someone she started savings accounts for each of her children at birth, and I guess she just kept adding to them over the years. But what happened? She forget about them?"

"Highly unlikely," Carol said. She laughed. "You didn't get the cane but you got the coins and now you have this. And there must be bankbooks for Victor and Lillian too. I wonder if they got them."

"I'll have to ask."

"But how did this one turn up *here*? There's something fishy about all this."

"There sure is, Carol, there sure is."

When Robbie heard this, panic struck and he went to his closet and took out the cane and held it. It calmed him, made his breathing smooth, but later, once he was in bed, even with Tofu up against him, it took him a long, long time to fall asleep.

The following day his father came home from work early and everything started up again in the kitchen.

"Why is he telling you this?" Carol said. "He's not thinking of letting you go, is he?"

"Could be," Tony said.

"My god. You've been working there for almost six years. How could he do this to you?"

"He's changed," Tony said. "Something's happened, he used to be fairly easy going, but now he's tough—on everybody, not just me."

"His business must be in trouble."

"Like many other businesses. It's just a terrible economy, that's all."

"Carol was quiet a minute then said, "How would we ever survive on what I make?"

"Let's just see what happens," Tony said, and went to the fridge for a beer.

Robbie was in the living room listening. He sniffed his fingers. There was never enough money, never!

ROBBIE

ROBBIE DECIDED TO GO to Brett's—and take the cane.

When he got there, he leaned it against the back porch. He and Brett began shooting arrows at Brett's new target when Buddy Lash rode up on his bike.

"Give me a turn!" he demanded.

You had to do what Buddy said or he'd punch you—*hard*.

Brett gave him the bow and arrows and Buddy grinned. "I could shoot you with this," he said. "Right through the heart."

Robbie was terribly nervous and went to his cane. It was vibrating strongly, saying words he couldn't understand.

Buddy took a few shots, barely hitting the target. When he saw what Robbie was holding he said, "What's that?"

"My cane," Robbie said.

"What are you, a crip or something?"

"No, I just like it."

"Give it to me."

"I can't, I'm not allowed."

"I said give it to me!" He went over to Robbie and snatched it out of his hand.

"Ow!" he suddenly yelled and dropped it on the ground.

"It bit me!"

"No!" Robbie said, "you just caught your hand in its teeth. They're very sharp."

"It bit me!" Buddy said again. "Look at my finger, it's bleeding!"

"I told you I couldn't give it to you," Robbie said as he picked it up. It was no longer buzzing.

"It bit my finger!" Buddy said. "I'll get you for this! I'll wreck that stupid cane!"

Robbie and Brett quickly ran to the house, up the steps of the porch, hurried inside and locked the door.

"It bit him," Brett said, breathing hard.

"No. I mean I don't think so…"

"I think it did. It must be magical."

"Maybe," Robbie said. He too was out of breath, and he thought of the buzzing he'd felt and the voices. "The cane will protect you," Grammy had said, and he knew she was right.

At school the following day Buddy Lash wasn't there.

In the schoolyard at recess, Marysue Boston, a girl in Buddy's class, told Robbie what had happened.

Buddy was walking his pit bull Rocky yesterday, when it suddenly turned on him, biting his leg. "It wouldn't let go," said Marysue. "He screamed and screamed but the pit bull just wouldn't let go. His father came out of the house with his rifle and shot it dead."

"While it was still biting?" Brett asked.

"That's right. And Buddy was crying and his father had

to pry the dog's jaws apart."

"How do you know all this?" Robbie said.

"Paul Collins saw it happen." Paul was thirteen and lived next door to Buddy.

Robbie and Brett had hated that dog and were glad he was dead. But why had he turned on Buddy?

"Well where is Buddy now?" Brett asked.

"In Riverside Hospital," Marysue said. "They had to sew him all up."

Robbie thought of how Buddy had said he'd destroy the cane. Could the cane have heard that, got into Rocky's head and made him attack? Impossible, he thought. Wolves have ears but canes with wolf's heads don't. But do they have…spirits? Had it *sensed* Buddy's words?

At home he changed into his play clothes and sniffed his fingers, then picked up the cane and took it outside. He wondered if he should keep it out here somewhere, maybe in the garden shed? Then it suddenly started up and he heard *bad boy don't let you can't—*

He took a deep breath, then dropped the cane on the grass and the voices faded away.

He heard a croaking then, looked up, and saw a bird on a branch of the maple tree next to the house. Like the one he had seen before, a bird like Grip! Like the one Brett had seen!

He picked up the cane, which was silent now, and hurried back to the house. The bird left the tree and followed him, crying out.

Inside, he put the cane in the mudroom and went to his room.

He was starting to have an asthma attack and quickly used

his breather. I'm okay! he said to himself. The cane had nothing to do with the dog attacking Buddy and I'm okay!

On the school bus the following morning there was talk of Buddy, but Robbie was lost in thoughts of the argument his parents had before they left for work.

About money again. His mother accused his father of being a spendthrift and drinking too much, the same old stuff. His father, as always, denied it.

His father *did* drink too much but at least he didn't use drugs. Robbie saw horrible things on TV about people who did. Opioids, heroin, fentanyl…people *died* from them. Alcohol could kill you too, but not as fast—unless you drank a whole lot of it all at once.

"If you lose your job, then what?" his mother had said. "*Then* what?"

His father shrugged. "I'll find another one."

Divorce, Robbie thought. *That terrible word. Divorce.*

He thought of it all day long and asked himself: could the Wolf maybe help? Keep his father from drinking so much? He had never mentioned a word of this drinking to Brett. It was a family secret, a very embarrassing one.

When school was finally out and the bus let him off at his house, he went right to his room. His parents were still at work and he sniffed his fingers and held his cat and said, "Tofu, what can I do? I found the box of coins and the passbook, what more can I do?"

Then he suddenly thought: I can sell the Wolf. It has to be worth big money.

He took the cane out of the closet and all at once it felt different. It wasn't buzzing at first then suddenly came alive with a stream of angry words he couldn't make out except for *bad*. He knew as he took it downstairs that he needed it to make himself feel good. And Grammy had warned him never to sell it or give it to anyone else...

As he held it now and felt its buzz, he suddenly knew again that his father was right in what he was doing, his mother was wrong. Then *Grammy!* he thought. *This is what Grammy would think!* Her thoughts were coming through the cane. *So what if he places bets on horses and sports? So what?* No, no! Robbie said to himself.

He heard the mudroom door shut and went through the kitchen and there was his father. "Hey Rob, I'm glad you're here," he said with a grin. "I'm off to a hockey game and I want you to come along. Does that sound good?"

A hockey game meant gambling and Robbie said, "I have homework to do."

"We'll be back in plenty of time for that."

"But what about dinner?"

"I'll leave your mother a note. We'll get hot dogs there and chips and ice cream bars and everything."

Beer, Robbie thought. *He would drink lots of beer.*

"Come on, kid," Tony said. "You only live once. You love hockey games, right?"

He didn't, he hated sports, but to please his father he always said he liked them. "I guess I'll go," he said.

"Great! Let me write that note."

Robbie insisted on taking his cane along.

"Why?" his father asked.

"It makes me feel good."

His father shrugged. "Okay" he said, "but I won't let you take it into the game."

"How come?"

"I don't want people to ask any questions about it."

"Oh."

When they parked outside the arena his father said, "We'll put the cane in the trunk. That gold head must look mighty appealing to thieves."

The game was half over, the home team (the Ramblers) was losing, and Robbie was eating a hot dog when a man he'd never seen before came over and talked to his father. Robbie didn't understand it all but it seemed to have to do with money. Money again! The man looked very serious, almost angry. When he left, Robbie asked about him.

"Just someone I know," Tony said.

"Was he mad at you?"

Tony grinned. "Now what made you think that?"

"He looked mad."

"Nah," Tony said, "that's just the way he is. Hey, beer over here!"

But then in the parking lot after the game, the man came up to them as Robbie took his cane out of the trunk. He didn't like this man, he was scared of him. And the cane didn't like him either. It began to vibrate.

"Another loss," the man said. "When are you going to pay up?"

"I need a couple of weeks," Tony said.

"Oh no," the man said. "No way." Then he looked at Robbie and said, "What's that?"

"My grandmother's cane," Robbie said.

"Let me see it. It looks like its head is gold."

"I can't give it to you," Robbie said, and the man said, "Let me see it!" and grabbed it out of his hand.

"Ow!" he said, and threw the cane down on the ground. "It bit me! I'm bleeding!"

"I told you—" Robbie said, picking it up.

"It bit me!"

"You just caught your hand on one of its teeth," Tony said.

The man shook his head. "No, it wasn't just that." He was frowning hard.

"Two weeks," Tony said and the man said, "Yeah, all right," and walked away.

Tony laughed. "He thought the cane bit him."

"It does that sometimes," Robbie said. "To people it doesn't like."

"You can't really believe that," Tony said.

"I do."

"The stuff my mother put in your head," Tony said.

CAROL

HER FACE WAS STERN when Tony and Robbie came through the door. "How much did you blow?" she asked.

"Not much. You win some and lose some, Carol."

"You've been drinking."

"Two beers," Tony said."

"With Robbie in the car."

"They didn't affect me at all."

Carol sighed and shook her head. "Hopeless," she said, and Robbie felt dreadful.

"Did you get enough to eat?" his mother asked.

He nodded yes. "I have homework to do now," he said. "Come on, Tofu."

With the cane in his hand and Tofu following, he climbed the stairs. When he reached the top he heard his mother say, "Jenkins called while you were gone. He did not sound happy."

"What now?" his father said.

"He wants you to call him."

"Now?" At this time of night?"

"Yes."

Tony made the call and Robbie heard him saying, "What?

I thought it was tomorrow. Yes. I understand. Okay. Yes, yes."

He turned off the phone and said to Carol, "I missed an appointment."

"Again?"

"I thought it was tomorrow. I would never have gone to that game today otherwise."

"Oh Tony."

"I don't know how it happened. I could have sworn it wasn't today."

"That's the second one this week."

"I know, I know. And this was a big one. I'll call them tomorrow and set up another time. Jenkins actually threatened me."

"Oh god."

"That jerk."

"But it *was* your fault."

"My fault or not, I'm going to look around for another job."

"You're not going to quit, are you?"

"No, but I'll start to look. People are just not buying. It's the lousy economy, can I be blamed for that?"

"No, but you *can* be blamed for missing appointments. What did you have to drink at lunch?"

"Let's not start that again."

"And you just won't stop gambling."

"Okay, okay."

Robbie felt his breathing contract. He went into his room and squeezed the cane, felt a mild buzz, and instantly felt better. "Everything will work out, Tofu," he said. "I know it will."

He had only gone to his father's office a couple of times, but could still picture Mr. Jenkins at his desk. He didn't like Mr. Jenkins, he seemed mean. *He has to change his mind about Daddy,* he thought. *Maybe the cane can make him change his mind,* and he squeezed it hard.

ROBBIE

THAT SUNDAY, AS ALWAYS, he went to church with Aunt Lillian. The woman with the yellow turban and golden rings in her ears was there again and Lillian said hello to her.

"Mrs. Carney," Robbie said.

"That's right, and she is filled with spirit. She has powers."

"Powers," Robbie repeated softly. "You told me she can see the future."

"She can. I gave her a key to Grammy's house. She's gone there several times to look for certain objects that are magical."

"Was she there last Tuesday?"

"Tuesday? Yes, I believe she was. I've just not been able to bring myself to go there yet, it will make me incredibly sad."

So that's whose footsteps I heard, Robbie thought. *That's whose face I saw in the upstairs window.*

"There are good spirits, Robbie, but bad ones too. She knows how to banish the bad ones."

"Oh," Robbie said.

They went to the cemetery again and Lillian knelt and

prayed at her mother's grave. And Robbie seemed to hear voices far away, but couldn't make out what they said.

When Lillian let him off at his house, the first thing he heard when he came through the door was his mother saying, "I feel terrible about what happened to him, but it's a reprieve." He didn't know what the word "reprieve" meant, but it had to be good.

His mother was on the living room couch and his father was in his easy chair. He said, "Did something bad happen?"

"Daddy's boss, Mr. Jenkins, fell off his ladder and hit his head while he was cleaning gutters and he's in a coma."

"Oh. That means he's not awake?"

"That's right, he's in Riverview. They don't know when he'll wake up."

"That's too bad," Robbie said, and he felt his stomach tighten.

"Mr. Jarvis will run the show while Jenkins is gone," his father said.

"Oh," Robbie said.

"Mrs. Jenkins called from Riverview," his mother said. "She told us a big black bird came right at Mr. Jenkins' head and when he tried to fight it off, he fell."

"Oh," Robbie said again. "I'm going to change my clothes," he said.

He went up to his room, Tofu following him. He took the cane out of his closet and thought: It helped. But not the way he thought it would, he thought it would help his father stop drinking or make good sales, but instead... And he wondered: had the cane made Buddy's pit bull go mad and attack? Had it sent the bird at Mr. Jenkins' head? Like Grip but not Grip, Grip was dead! "Of course birds have spirits," Aunt Lillian said. "All creatures have spirits, Robbie."

But do *things* have spirits? he wondered. Do *canes* have spirits? Maybe so, if they were made by wizards.

From downstairs he heard his father say, "Jarvis won't push. He understands the situation."

"You are very lucky, Tony," his mother said.

JEFF

THE MIGRAINE HAD PRETTY much vanished when, to Jeff's dismay, Richard showed up. He'd hoped that the visions had run their course. This was getting to be ridiculous.

Richard opened his mouth to speak but Jeff cut him off. "I know what you're going to say, but just listen to me for a minute before you start. One time I was in a real slump that lasted for weeks and decided to go to a writers' conference, hoping to get myself moving again. I had never been to a conference before and didn't know what to expect. Well, this one was run by a college professor, a 'literary' writer who'd had a number of novels published by 'good' companies. He warned us not to waste our time writing what he called 'trash.' Then he told us that what he does when his spring semester ends is pack a bag with cheesy detective novels and go to his rustic cabin and read them one after another to help him unwind. He *loves* them. Well, *somebody* has to write them. What a hypocrite!"

"You mean to tell me even colleges have hypocrites?" Richard said. "Amazing!" and he laughed.

Jeff said, "I'm just an ordinary writer writing for ordinary people. There are thousands of writers like me out there, and how few of them make it as far as I have, let alone to the top? How many excellent painters, musicians, actors, dancers, comedians or *anything* ever make it to the top? I'm proud of how far I've come, of the small reputation I've earned."

"As an entertainer. But you want more ."

"I did once, but now I have to forget about that."

"And so you keep dying, bit by bit."

"No, I keep *living*. I get *paid* for what I do, but it's more than that. I *need* my writing. If I stop, I'm afraid I *will* die."

"I don't want you to stop, I just want you to change."

"But I don't want to."

"I think you do."

"Oh really? Do you know how hard that is? Some writers are lucky and see the whole story right from the start. They actually use *outlines*. I've tried, but they always fall flat or run in a different direction. I have to build the story day by day, piece by piece, and it always has holes—I call it my "Swiss cheese" draft—which I need to fill in later. As for that professor I told you about, I never knew his working habits but do know he only wrote "serious" novels—exactly what he wanted to write—and suffered a fatal heart attack standing in line for a Broadway play. He was sixty-four years old."

"Only five years older than you are now. How tragic. But I think he was right, you have to get out of the ghetto."

"The ghetto? Tell it to Henry James. His *Turn of the Screw*—"

"But he made a foray from mainstream into the ghetto and what I'd like you to do is the opposite of that. Or maybe you've given up on the mainstream completely."

"Maybe so. And what's it to you?"

"I'm just giving you something to think about."

"I get it. But see…"

Richard's right ear was shining and then it was gone. Then his forehead began to fade and Jeff said, "Wait, don't go, I have more to say."

"My time has run out. Sorry."

ROBBIE

THE WEATHER TURNED COLDER. More snow. For weeks Aunt Lillian didn't go to her mother's grave. She finally went back to the old house though, cleaning up and changing things around.

Robbie went with her twice. He asked for a few of the figurines on the library shelves but she didn't give them to him. But the second time he went he gave her something shocking.

"Where in the world did you ever find these?" she said in amazement. "This is incredible!"

"In the bottom drawer of Grammy's desk," Robbie said.

"These bankbooks are still valid—and there's a lot of money in them!"

"I know. I remember Grammy giving one to my father right before she died" (this of course was a lie he'd just made up), "and I thought there must be others for you and Uncle Victor, so I looked for them."

"And you were right! Just wait until Victor finds out about this!"

"Can I have those figurines now?"

"Of course you can. Of course."

———— 96 ————

Buddy Lash came back to school. He had a limp, so he couldn't run fast anymore, which was good news for Robbie and Brett. But Robbie took no chances; he never carried The Golden Wolf when Buddy was on the street.

Mr. Jenkins had still not woken up. Robbie's father was making some excellent sales and seemed much happier. He rarely went out to the Rusty Bucket and drank very little at home.

One day he came through the mudroom door and said to Robbie, "Christmas is coming up and Mr. Jarvis gave me a present—two tickets to a Ramblers game. What say we go tonight. They're playing the Comets, who are really good."

"Oh, sure," Robbie said, but thought: he'll place a bet. He'd been staying away from that lately. But soon he heard his father on the phone and that's what he was doing. And it sounded like lots of money.

Brett collected sports cards: baseball, football, basketball and hockey. Robbie gave him a call and asked, "Who's the best player on the Comets' hockey team?" Without hesitating Brett said, "Stanley Cartright."

"Can you bring his card over here real quick?"

"Okay, but why?"

"I'll explain when you get here."

When Brett arrived, they went to Robbie's room and Robbie took his cane out of the closet. He suddenly heard a jumble of voices, a web of confusion. He had Brett put the card on his desk and held the cane over it.

"What are you doing?" Brett said.

"I'm asking my cane to give Stanley Cartright a bad game tonight."

"You really think that will work?"

"Maybe, I don't know."

"You're really weird sometimes," Brett said.

"I believe the Wolf has powers," Robbie said.

He held it tighter and the voices grew louder, but no more comprehensible. His father couldn't lose this bet, he just couldn't. He squeezed the cane again then gave the card back to Brett. "Thanks a lot for bringing this to me."

"No problem. I wish I could go to the game with you, but my father doesn't like hockey."

Robbie thought of asking Brett to come along with him, but what if his father started drinking? "My father only got two tickets, they were a gift," he said. "But the game's on TV."

"I'll watch it and see how Cartright does," Brett said. "He's really good. And I don't think this stuff you've done with the cane will hurt him at all."

They went downstairs, and Robbie left his cane in the mudroom and said goodbye to Brett. He wasn't hearing voices anymore.

When it was time to go, his father said, "You're not taking that thing to the game again, are you? Remember what happened last time?"

"It bit that man."

"Well…I'm not sure about that, it might have been an accident. So why are you taking it?"

"Like I told you before, it makes me feel good."

"You mean in your chest or stomach?"

"All over."

His father frowned. "You'll have to leave it in the trunk again."

"I know that," Robbie said.

On the drive, Robbie held the cane close to his chest and heard the voices far away. In the parking lot Tony said, "In the trunk it goes."

They went inside and found their seats. The game had only been going a couple of minutes when Robbie said to his father, "Where's Cartright?"

The man on the other side of him said, "He tripped getting out of his car in the parking lot and sprained his ankle."

Robbie breathed a big sigh of relief. The favor he had asked of the cane had come true.

Without Cartright, the Comets were out of synch and the Ramblers won. Tony, who only had one beer, was overjoyed.

When they got back home, he said to Carol, "We won— in more ways than one."

"Don't tell me. You said you weren't going to gamble anymore."

"Well, everyone slips sometimes."

"This is the last time," Carol said.

"Hey, I'm doing great at work again. Two sales this week and more on the way."

"I worry, Tony, I worry."

Up in his room with Tofu Robbie thought: Cartright tripped getting out of his car, it was an accident. But what had *caused* the accident? The cane. He knew it was the cane. Just showing it that card… But how did that work? "You will learn how to use it," Grammy said when she gave it to him, and he guessed he was doing just that.

JEFF

JEFF HAD BEEN TOLD by one of the doctors he'd gone to that meditation might help with the migraines. It didn't, but he found that he liked it because it made him relax and temporarily escape his problems. So after his morning work he would usually sit at the kitchen table, hands on his thighs, eyes closed, and inhale calmly, exhale calmly, focusing on the word "peace."

On this particular day he'd been meditating for almost ten minutes (and getting quite hungry) when he heard a car in the driveway and opened his eyes. It was Sandra's car.

He was so glad to see her and opened the kitchen door.

"Well look at you!" she said. "A beard!"

"Do you like it?"

"I'm not sure. It makes you look older. You look kind of like Santa Claus."

"Too bad it isn't Christmas."

"It *is* Christmas!"

"What?"

"Wow, you really have lost track of time."

"I haven't looked at the calendar for days."

"Well even in your fictional world, it's Christmas. So give me a fuzzy kiss."

He did.

"That'll take getting used to," she said.

"Don't worry, I'll shave it off before I leave here."

Sandra was Jewish, but celebrated Christmas. Her husband, Larry, had not been Jewish and her daughters loved the holiday and so they always had a tree with presents under it. "And here is a present for you," she said, withdrawing something from her coat.

A bag of homemade rugula. "Perfect!" he said. "I was just about to make lunch. No turkey, I'm afraid. Will you settle for BLTs?"

"My favorite sandwich."

"I thought you might show up pretty soon, it seems like weeks since I've seen you."

"It has been. Let me take a look around and see if there are any calamities."

She inspected the place and said, "Looks the same, except for the dirty dishes in the sink. And the unmade bed. And the Smith Corona. How long has it been since you've used that thing?"

"Years. But I kind of like it. It makes me more careful about what I write. And I like the clacking sound."

"You would," Sandra said with a smile. "Smells like you're still smoking."

She had urged him to quit a while ago. He had quit three times before, with Allison, but always relapsed. "Once I finish my book I'll make a concerted effort," he said.

He was terribly happy that Sandra had come. No phone

and the post office didn't deliver mail down here, so there wasn't any way for him to know when she would appear.

"So how are the kids?" he asked.

"Amelia's coming home today."

"She's doing well in school?" Amelia was the older one, now twenty, in her sophomore year of college. She was good-looking but no beauty, an outgoing chatterbox who could talk your head off—about almost anything.

"She's doing great."

"And Becky?" Becky was still at home, in her last year of high school. A quiet kid, who *was* a beauty and also a spectacular cook. Once she went off to college Jeff and Sandra might try living together, but weren't sure about that yet.

"Let me go get your mail," Sandra said.

"You brought my mail?"

"I did."

She went out to her car again and came back with a shopping bag full. "Most of it's junk, I'm afraid."

"I'll check it later," Jeff said. "Just put it over there in the corner."

She took off her jacket and sat at the kitchen table. He brought out a pan and started to fry some bacon, happy as could be, when he suddenly noticed a small blank spot in his vision. Not *now*, he thought. It wouldn't affect his sandwich-making, and so he decided not to tell Sandra about it. But then his hands started to tremble.

"You're having a migraine," she said.

"I am. Just a small one."

"On Christmas Day. What luck."

"It will pass pretty quickly—I hope."

He finished making the sandwiches, took a bag of chips from a cabinet above the sink and some apple juice from the fridge. He put coffee on, then sat at the kitchen table across from her. The dregs of the migraine were fading. Richard had not appeared, thank god, and Jeff's hands had calmed down.

"It's over," Sandra said. "How often do you have them?"

"I'm into a bad stretch right now."

"Do they keep you from working?"

He thought of Richard again. "No," he said, "but sometimes they throw me off stride and make me unsure of how to proceed."

"You've always had that problem, even without any migraines."

"You're right. It must be nice to reach a sticky place and eventually see one way to go. I always see a dozen ways to go and have to pick the best one."

"Are you always right?"

"Not always, no. Now let's just forget this stuff and eat."

She bit into her sandwich. "You make a great BLT. Always have and always will."

"My only culinary feat," Jeff said. He decided not to mention Richard, afraid she would think he had gone completely off the rails.

She said, "I hesitated coming, didn't want to interrupt your work. But I did, I can tell by the way you act, I'm getting that half-brain thing."

"That's just the remains of the migraine," Jeff said. "You can come any time you want." (Of course he didn't mean it.)

"So bring me up to speed."

"Well for one thing, Don Leonard called yesterday," she said.

His editor. He had given him Sandra's number in case he needed to get in touch. "About what?"

"Just to see how you're doing. I guess he's getting anxious since you haven't sent him anything. I told him I didn't know how you were but I planned to see you today. How *are* you doing?"

"Oh you know me. I'm one of those guys who laughs his way through life with a crematorium card in his wallet."

"Seriously."

"I'm fine."

"You look a little thinner."

"There's no scale in here."

"Your work is going well?"

"It's going okay."

"You always say that."

"I guess I do."

"Maybe you can send Don a chapter or two and make him relax a bit."

"I don't have anything ready yet. But why don't you call him and tell him it's coming along."

"Okay, I will."

"I wish I could be with you and the girls today," he said. "For a good old-fashioned Jewish Christmas."

She laughed. But he knew she must be thinking of other Christmases when Larry was still alive and her girls were small. The excitement and joy and happiness of that.

They finished their BLTs and chips and juice, drank coffee and ate dessert. "Delicious," he said. "You are the world's best rugula maker."

"I have to agree," she said. "Well listen, Santa, I have to get home, Amelia might already be there. I'm dying to see her."

"Can't you stay just a little bit longer?"

"Not now, some other time."

They stood, they hugged, they kissed.

"Thank you so much for coming," he said. "But don't wait for another holiday. And tell both of the kids I love them to pieces."

After she left, he felt empty. He smoked another cigarette and lay back on the couch. Christmas. I missed it! he thought, and dozed.

In his dream he was talking to Allison, then found himself outside in a barren landscape with dried-up evergreens—dead Christmas trees. No lights or ornaments, just sand, a desert, and heat, brutal heat. Then he woke up to jagged bright colors thinking, Why Allison, why not Sandra? and Richard was there, his left shoulder sparkling with silver dots.

"So now you come," Jeff said.

"Well, I figured it wouldn't do to start our dialog again while Sandra was here, especially since she can't see or hear me. She might get the impression that you are a little…shall we say, strange? She seems like a very good person, by the way."

"She's wonderful," Jeff said.

"Her husband died."

"Of a heart attack."

"How awful."

"And she started drinking after that. We met at AA."

"I know."

"What *don't* you know?"

"I know that from time to time you wished you had children. You'd have taught them to catch a ball, ride a bike, swim, fish."

"All those wonderful things," Jeff said. "But balance that against earaches, sore throats, fevers, broken bones... I couldn't do it."

Not having kids had torn apart his relationship with Allison. She wanted them so badly and he didn't want them at all. "You and your precious writing," she said to him. "Nothing gets in the way of that, does it?"

"I'm on a roll right now," he said. "I can't have any interference."

More arguments—not just over this, of course—and they finally split up. "You put your writing ahead of human beings," Allison said.

It was true. And she now had two kids, two boys, with her second husband, who was a high school principal.

"You regret not having children," Richard said. "That's why you write so many stories about them."

"Could be. But my children don't always turn out the way I want them to. They have more fears and neuroses than I'd like."

"And you can't change that?"

"The person shapes itself in spite of what I do."

"How odd."

"All my people do that. You have something in mind and then when you're writing it, things mutate. But that's a big part of the fun. It can be maddening and frustrating, but it's always exciting. I never know where I'm going from day to day. It's always an adventure."

"And no regrets."

"Oh no, I regret a lot of things. I regret not having a best-seller."

"You feel you deserved one."

"Of course. You already know what happened, I'm sure."

"The movie. But tell me again. I may have missed some details."

"I'm sure you didn't, but, if you really want me to. I had a friend with Hollywood connections who said he loved one of my unpublished manuscripts and would show it around Hollywood."

"Unpublished?" Richard said. "I didn't remember *that* detail. Didn't you know that was *dangerous*?"

"I didn't. Back then I naively thought there were ethics in Hollywood."

"So what happened?"

"The guy showed my manuscript around and nobody bit."

"This was your novel called *Green*, about a professional golfer."

"Right. Then two years later a movie came out, and it was my story—which still hadn't been published. One of the readers my guy had shown it to stole it! The movie got great reviews and made tons of money. I was enraged, but what could I do? Sue the movie company? How much would that cost? They of course changed the title and certain incidents enough to say that any similarities were coincidental. I felt actually sick for days. They'd stabbed me in the heart! How could anyone *do* such a thing? I lay awake night after night. I have a sick feeling even now when I think about it. Of course once the movie was made, my agent would no longer handle the book."

"Of course."

"I tried different agents and editors. The response was always the same: "It's too much like that wonderful movie, *The Long Drive.*"

"It's still never been published."

"That's right. One of my best books, and never been published."

"This all happened when you were scratching like mad to make a living."

"You know about that. Of course you do. Why do I bother talking to you?"

"You tell me. There must be a reason."

"Well, I don't know what it is."

"I think you do. Any other regrets?"

"Concerning my work?"

"Not necessarily. Any regrets at all."

"Well here's a big one, then. I regret that our planet is doomed."

"Come now."

"It is, of course. Aside from the threat of nuclear annihilation, which I and most other people have lived with forever, there's the bigger threat of overpopulation. In the time of Jesus, two thousand years ago, three hundred million people lived on this planet. The whole *world* had fewer people than America has now. Imagine all that *space*. Imagine what the *air* was like. By 1900 it had grown to one point six *billion*—with plenty of factories spewing their smoke. Today it's at *seven* billion and increasing by the minute. It's totally unsustainable. We've poisoned the water and air, created catastrophic climate change, the oil and gas are running out and unless population drastically declines, it's all over. And what are the chances of that?"

"You could write a story about a plague that kills almost everybody."

"It's already been done, many times, which I'm sure you know."

"And you think what you're writing now is *original?*"

"Of course not, but it works for me."

"And a plague wouldn't work as well, or even better?"

"I don't know, but I do know this. Even if we stop climate change, we're all polluted with foreign man-made chemicals. Every bite of food we eat, every breath we take— our cells are swarming with them. Babies have them *in utero*. One out of sixty children born today has autistic symptoms. A few decades ago, it was one in ten thousand. Why has this happened? Pretty soon the earth will be done in by disabilities. I'd like to shake everybody and say, Wake up! Can't you see what's going on?"

"Why don't you, then?"

"Oh, sure. You want to show me how?"

"That's funny. I show *you*."

"Funny to you, but not to me."

Richard was silent a moment then said, "Let me ask you

something. Do you think that the Ice Age was created by human beings?"

"Of course not."

"Do you think that people back then thought the world was ending?"

"I don't know what people back then thought—if there even *were* people—but we *are* causing climate change. And people back then didn't have to deal with islands of trash the size of Texas in their oceans—or oceans dying from excess acid."

"So what you do," Richard said, "is escape from what you see as this ruined world through your fantasy stories."

"Exactly. They're my *retreat*. I create my *own* world and reside in it—and hope that my readers reside in it too. What a relief from reality! In a way, I play god. I bring rivers (which flood sometimes), forests (which burn sometimes) and towns (which flood and burn sometimes) to life, and best of all I bring *people* to life. Not without a struggle, of course."

"Your cast of characters."

"They aren't characters to me, they're *people*."

"And every one of them is you."

"You're right. No matter how loathsome they are, they're all variations of me."

"You opt out of the real world for their sake."

"Maybe so. But what about you? Are you real? Or just a branch of my imagination? A *character*."

"Could be."

A book Jeff was reading sat on the end table: *Poltergeists, Spirits and Familiars*. He suddenly picked it up and threw it at Richard. It went right through his chest and landed on the floor.

"Does that answer your question?" Richard said. "Bye now."

His shoulder pulsed with blinding silver light and then he was gone.

ROBBIE

BEFORE HE AWOKE ON Christmas Day, he had a strange dream of a Christmas tree with dead brown needles and no lights or ornaments. But when he got up and went downstairs his parents were there in the living room drinking coffee and the tree was fine as always, lit up with presents under it.

He liked all the presents he got but especially a couple of new computer games (one about capturing wild animals, one about exploring an Egyptian pyramid—his mother wouldn't allow him to have any games containing violence) and a box of his favorite chocolates. He had to go to church with Aunt Lillian, but the day was bitterly cold and she didn't go to the cemetery.

His mother had gone to a neighbor's house for lunch and his father was home alone. As he passed his study his father was on the computer. Checking listings? Or placing a bet? How could he ever get him to stop? Every once in a while he won, which made him bet again, and then he would lose all he'd won and more.

A few days later he heard his mother say downstairs, "I just can't do it, Tony, I have to pay our mortgage and bills. You said you wouldn't ask me again."

They had separate bank accounts. His mother felt this was absolutely necessary.

"I have to hold this guy off," his father said. "If it wasn't for Christmas, I could've done it."

"Blame Christmas."

"Okay, okay. But if I don't pay this guy right now, I'm in real trouble. He doesn't mess around."

His mother didn't respond for a minute then said, "How much do you need?"

A week later, her car stopped working and she had to have it towed.

"Transmission," the mechanic at Atlas Motors said.

So Tony had to drive her to work in the mornings and pick her up in the afternoons until the car was fixed.

"We're broke again," she said.

"I have some good sales coming up," he said.

"Where have I heard that before?"

Robbie was frantic. No matter how bad things got, his father would never stop gambling and they would never have enough money. In his room he held the Wolf and asked it, *What can I do?* and the voices began. The typical scatter of words that he couldn't make out, then suddenly: *My cellar.*

Robbie had never been to Grammy's cellar. He had hardly even seen it since its door was always closed, except for one time when his father was cleaning up for the furnace man. It was terribly scary down there, but now he had to go.

He would go with Brett. He talked to him and Brett said, "I don't like that house."

"Neither do I, but I have to go back to it."

"Why?"

"I have to find something else."

"You always have to find something else."

"You're right, I do. Please, Brett, it won't take long."

"Will you buy me a frappe at Lonny's if I go?"

"It's a deal."

He left Tofu home this time; he couldn't have her running off again as she had before. But he took the cane.

As they rode on their bikes Brett said, "Look up. That bird is following us."

The bird they had seen before, the one like Grip. When they got to Grammy's house it settled into the large oak tree that stood beside the west wall.

They leaned their bikes against the porch again and went up the steps. Robbie inserted the key in the lock and opened the door and again the smell. "Come on, Brett, get in here."

"I hate this place," Brett said, but he stepped inside. "If I hear footsteps again, I'm outta here."

"I found out that was just Mrs. Carney," Robbie said.

"Who's that?"

"This medium. She's a friend of my aunt's."

"What's a medium?"

"Like a fortune teller. She was looking for magical stuff."

"And what are *you* looking for?" Brett asked.

"I don't really know."

They walked down the shadowy hallway and into the kitchen. The cellar door was on their right. Robbie pulled it open and there was another smell, dark, musty and damp. He clicked the light switch and a feeble bulb came on below.

His father had come every August to brush all the cobwebs away before the oil burner guy arrived for his annual maintenance. Robbie had gone with him once and had stood at the top of the steps—and had smelled that very same smell. "What's down there?" he had asked.

"Spiders," his father had answered.

"Are they poisonous?"

"No, just a nuisance with all their webs."

"Is anything else down there?"

"A lot of junk."

Robbie thought that this must be true. His father would have sold anything good, provided he could get it past Grammy.

"I'm not going down there," Brett said.

"Oh, come on."

"I'm not. I'll stay up here and keep watch."

"You wimp. The cane will protect us."

"Maybe, but I'm not going down there."

"Okay," Robbie said. "I'll go alone."

He held his cane tightly and started down the steps. They were black with age; he could just about see them. Right away he had to brush cobwebs off his face. As soon as the oil burner guy was through the spiders resumed their work.

At the foot of the steps the cobwebs were dense and his

jacket was covered with them. The spiders weren't dangerous, his father said. They could probably bite, he didn't know, but they had no poisons. He hated them, they gave him the shivers, and he wondered: did they have souls? They were alive, so they probably did. And mosquitoes too? If so, their souls must be really small.

The cellar walls were made of huge dark stones and its floor was dirt; no one had cemented it in all these years. If I had this house I'd cement it right off, Robbie thought. And I'd paint the walls white. He looked around for another light switch but couldn't find one. There had to be one, but where was it?

It was cold down here; he could see his breath. His father had set the heat very low just to keep the pipes from freezing. Dim light seeped through a narrow, dingy window past the huge furnace. It fell on dozens of chairs and tables and wooden boxes stacked on top of each other. An ornate disassembled bed leaned against one wall. All this belongs to Aunt Lillian now, he thought.

How can I ever find what I'm supposed to look for? he wondered. And what *am* I supposed to look for?

The furnace came on just then so hard that he jumped and dropped the cane. He picked it up again and went deeper, fighting off cobwebs. One of them got on his lips and he made a disgusted face and shuddered as he brushed it away.

Who will get all this stuff? he wondered. Would Aunt Lillian throw it out? Would she ever come down here? Had she ever *been* down here?

All at once he heard a scratching sound and held his breath. There was something down here with him—an animal! He looked all around, but couldn't see anything. He heard it again and then, in the shadows under a table against the far wall, he saw it.

A cat! What in the world was it doing down here? How did it get in? A good thing he hadn't brought Tofu, this cat looked... Wait a second, this wasn't a cat, it was a rat!

A huge one, bigger than Tofu! He shuddered and thought, I have to get out of here! Right now!

He spotted a piece of brick on the floor, picked it up and threw it. The rat disappeared in a hole.

Aunt Lillian would need to have the rat holes fixed. Why hadn't Grammy done it? A big job, the cellar was huge. Maybe she had asked his father. He'd know how to do it but probably never would.

"What are you doing down there?" Brett called from above. "It's creepy here, I want to go home."

"I can't leave yet," Robbie said. "There's something I have to find."

"Well hurry up."

Where, where? Robbie thought, then he thought: *Look up.*

It wasn't a voice, exactly, but he heard it in his head. Look up.

He started to look at the cellar's far end, where the doors to the outside were, and saw nothing. He walked all the way to where the rat had been, holding the cane in front of him. If that rat ever came again he'd hit it with the Wolf's head—hard! He couldn't get close to two of the walls because of all the furniture and stuff. If only he had more light!

Look up, he heard again. He did, and then... Ga*zorp!*

A small catch over his head. He was too short to reach it,

so he dragged a small end table over and climbed on top of it. He reached up, twisted the catch; a little door flopped open and hung down. He felt around inside the opening and his hand hit something: a box. It was pretty small, and he took it out of the hole.

It was made of metal—brass, he thought. He shut the door to the hole, twisted the catch to hold it in place, got down from the table, took up his cane, and climbed the stairs to the kitchen. His hat and jacket were covered with cobwebs. He turned the cellar light off, put the box down on the kitchen floor and brushed the cobwebs off. Not easy, they were sticky.

"You found what you were looking for," Brett said.

"I did," Robbie said. He placed the box on the kitchen table and sat in one of its chairs.

He opened the box. There was a letter there, quite old, a bunch of other papers, and a little blue velvet sack.

"What's in that thing?" Brett said.

"Let's see," Robbie said, and reached inside—and, to his complete surprise, came up with Grammy's diamond wedding ring.

He frowned. "I don't understand… I saw it on her finger in the coffin. How could it possibly be here?"

Weird," Brett said. "But maybe the one on her finger was a fake," he said. "Maybe this is the real one."

"Yeah, maybe. My mother was really upset when she saw it on Grammy's hand. I guess she wanted it, but my father insisted that she be buried with it."

"How come?"

"I don't know. But this has to be the real one."

"What are you going to do with it? What will you tell your father?"

Robbie took a deep breath. "Look, I want you to take the box home with you and put it in your room until I can figure things out."

"Well...I don't know."

"I'll keep the ring and you take the box."

Brett's shoulders slumped. "But what if it has evil spirits in it?"

"I thought you didn't believe in spirits."

"Well, being here I maybe do."

"The box doesn't have any spirits."

"I hope not." Brett took the box from Robbie. "I'm freezing," he said. "Let's get out of here!"

When they reached Brett's house Robbie said, "Keep the box out of sight, then take it to your room when your parents aren't around. You won't have to keep it long."

"I sure hope not."

"You can read all the old stuff in it if you want."

"It looks real boring. Let's go to Lonny's for that frappe you promised me."

"Okay, I could use one too after all those creepy spiders."

After the frappes, Robbie went to his room with the cane, put it in the closet, and put the ring under some socks in his top bureau drawer.

This is the real ring, he thought, the one in the coffin is a fake. That would be so like Grammy. She'd think that his father would want the ring buried with her, so she had a fake ring made to fool him. She was not one to throw any money away.

That night, when they were eating supper, Robbie said, "Can I go back to Grammy's house again?"

"What for?" his father said. He was on his second beer.

"I left something there when Grammy was still alive, a little car. I forgot to take it when I went with you. It's for my talk in school tomorrow. I forgot I didn't have it."

"I'm too tired to go tonight."

"If you give me the key to the house, I'll go by myself."

"It's too dark out. And too cold."

"No, I'll be fine. I really need that car."

"Do your talk with something else," Tony said.

"I already told Ms. Hudson what I was doing."

"Oh, all right," Tony said, and he drank the rest of his beer.

"You better go with him," his mother said.

"Nah. He'll be all right."

"You'll come right back," his mother said.

"I will."

He went up to his room and put the bag with the ring in his pocket, then pedaled to Brett's. He had a headlight on his bike and also a red taillight.

"What's up?" Brett said.

"Just wanted to know if you looked through the stuff in the box."

"Not really," Brett said.

"Let's do it."

They went up to Brett's room. Its walls were covered with pictures of sports stars and superheroes…and a poster of Gordie the Gumshoe Groundhog with a cartoon balloon above his head that said "Ga*zorp!*" Robbie's walls held only three pictures, one of Tofu, one of Gordie, and one of Jack Be Nimble. The Jack Be Nimble was kind of embarrassing, but had been there his entire life and he knew he'd miss it if he took it down. Besides that, it glowed in the dark, which he found comforting.

Brett took the box from his closet and opened it up. Most of the stuff had to do with financial transactions they couldn't make sense of. But there was that letter...

Robbie read it out loud. The man who had written it said that he still loved Adelaide—Grammy's name!—knew that she loved their child, wished he'd been able to see him grow up, but it was not to be.

This puzzled Robbie. Why was it not to be? And what was this stuff about their child? The letter had not been signed.

"A real mystery!" Brett said.

Robbie stayed there for almost an hour, then went back home. When he entered the living room he said, "I couldn't find my car, but I found something else," and he took the velvet bag with the ring in it out of his pocket. "I was looking through all the desk drawers again and way in the back of one I found this."

He handed the bag to his father.

Tony opened it up and the ring fell into his palm. "What in the world?" he said. "It's Mother's wedding ring! But it was still right there on her finger, I made sure of that…"

"Maybe the one on her finger was a fake," Robbie said.

Tony laughed. "It wouldn't surprise me if she pulled a trick like that. I'll take this to Bill Scott's tomorrow and have him check it out. But without the car, what are you going to do about your talk?"

"I'll have to think of something," Robbie said.

He took an old coin that Grammy had given him once when she was handing out butterscotch. It was a large cent from 1812. "That's when we were fighting a war with Great Britain," he said in front of the class.

"Who won?" Jimmy Baker asked.

"The British burned the White House down but we burned Canadian places down so it kind of came out even," Robbie said.

ROBBIE

ROBBIE WENT SLEDDING THAT afternoon. Or, as they called it in Maine, "sliding." When he came inside and stood in the mudroom, he heard his mother's angry voice: "Without even letting me know," she said.

"You were at work," his father said. "I didn't want to bother you."

"You knew I wouldn't let you do it."

"Maybe, yeah. But look, just as we thought, it was real. She knew I'd have it buried with her so she made a fake. She wanted me to sell the real one. She knew I'd find it eventually."

"Or Victor or Lillian would."

"Victor doesn't want anything more to do with that house, and Lillian isn't ready to move in yet. Maybe she never *will* be ready."

"The ring really belongs to her," Carol said. 'The house and all its contents.' That's what it said in the will."

"Well, she'll never know about this."

Carol was shaking her head. "I still can't believe you sold it without consulting me."

"Did you want me to keep it? Would you actually wear my mother's wedding ring?"

"Of course not."

"Then what's the problem? Bill Scott made me an offer right away and I took it. I needed the money, Carol."

"And how much did he give you?"

"Five thousand."

"For a diamond that large? You should have gotten twice that much!"

"You expect him to pay retail for it? He has a business to run. And I'm in a tight spot."

"I'm tired of your tight spots! You already took my money and now you've sold that ring for half of what it's worth!"

Robbie felt sick to his heart. He thought maybe he should have kept the ring and hidden it somewhere. But he would never have found it in Grammy's house if not for the voice in his head. The voice had wanted him to help his father out by giving him the ring and he had done it. If he hadn't, who knows what might have happened?

"I've paid what I owe and that's the end of it," Tony said.

"I have heard that so many times," Carol said. "And your drinking is getting out of control again. You should go back to AA."

"I can't stand that bunch of coffee drinkers."

Robbie took off his coat and hat and hung them up, then took off his boots.

He was sure that giving the ring to his father was right, his father had needed the money. His mother was wrong to yell at him for selling it. After all, whose ring was it? But she was right to yell at him for drinking. If only he could stop!

He went up to his room, took the cane from the closet and whispered, "Help me, Wolf. Help my father stop drinking. Please!" Then, clutching his penis, he prayed to God.

His pleading seemed to work. Whether the Wolf or God or both had helped he didn't know, but for two whole weeks his father didn't touch a drop and seemed to have quit his gambling. His boss, Mr. Jenkins, was still recuperating from his fall, but his substitute, Mr. Jarvis, was happy with Tony's performance. "There's a regional sales conference starting on Wednesday," he said," and I'd like you to represent us."

"Wonderful," Carol said. "But can you keep from drinking for four days in that environment?"

"I'm on a roll," Tony said. "No problem."

"I don't trust conferences."

"But you trust me, right?" Tony said, and gave her a kiss on the cheek, then went outside to smoke.

If only he could quit *that* filthy habit, Carol thought, things would be—well, not perfect—but as good as they were ever going to get. Right at the moment, though, that was too much to ask.

JEFF

RICHARD WAS WEARING A corduroy jacket, a brown one, over a black T-shirt this time. "A typical writer's outfit," he said. "You probably look like this when you give a talk."

"You're spot on," Jeff said from the couch, "which doesn't surprise me at all."

"I dressed this way to present you with an idea," Richard said. "You told me you once wrote a novel under a pseudonym. So to make a fresh start, why not create a fake biography, fictionalize yourself. You could say you were one of eleven children, two of whom died of congenital heart disease and you have a bit of a problem yourself. Your family was very poor and lived in a slum. You were often so hungry you ate out of garbage cans. You wore your older siblings' hand-me-downs. Your shoes had holes in the soles and you had to cut cardboard inserts for them to keep from scraping your feet on the pavement. Your father was a drunk and your mother died of kidney disease when you were twelve. You stole, were caught and went to reform school. A kindly teacher there took you under her wing and straightened you out. You visit her in her nursing home every so often… And the best part is, you're only twenty-three!"

"Twenty-three! I can hardly remember when I was twenty-three."

"So much the better. Publishers love that stuff. The younger you are and the weirder you are, the better. You'll give yourself a strange name, maybe 'Dynamite,' or 'Pistol.' This is what you'll use for your real work."

Jeff sniffed. "My real work."

"That's right. A brand new author! Just twenty-three! A debut novel!"

"So you want me to have 'a fresh start'—which means I should turn myself into a character and promote myself. Turn into a PR man, exactly what I never wanted to be. Join the social network and all its banality."

"Why not? All people are actors anyway. When you give a talk, are you really *you*—or a pumped-up version of yourself? When you deal with Sandra or with anyone, you're not really the *real* you."

"I am and I'm not. But you want me to actually *lie*."

"You always do. Everyone does."

"Okay, you're right, but not to that extent. Most of those people get caught in their lies anyway."

"You don't really believe that."

"I do, and I'm not going to make a phony me to do what you call my 'real' work. I spend enough time in a fantasy world without that."

The airtight was dying down and he got up to feed it. And then on the way back he saw something strange. "The mirror reflects my image but not yours," he said.

Richard laughed. "I must be a vampire," he said.

"Very funny."

"To tell you the truth, it's a matter of conservation," Richard said.

"What do you mean?"

"It takes a lot of energy to create a reflection. I can't afford it."

"Your energy is in short supply?"

"It is. Observe my right cheek."

It suddenly turned transparent and Jeff saw rows of teeth.

"You see, the closer you get to my plan for you, the weaker I become."

"Wait a minute," Jeff said. "Are you trying to tell me you *cause* the migraines?"

"Ah, if only I could. But I have no control, I just appear— and disappear. I'm at the mercy of something, of what, I don't know. Let me put it this way. We're in a story, right? If so, who's writing it?"

"What do you mean?"

"Who's writing this stuff about you and me?"

"The Oversoul," I guess.

"Good answer," Richard said, and laughed.

Jeff said, "You're really messing with my head. But I guess that's the point."

"Maybe so. I need you to think along different lines."

"Goddamn it, I am!"

He suddenly noticed that Richard's nose had disappeared and now his chest was fading. Just before his mouth fell apart, he said, "You're catching on."

CAROL

THE MORNING OF THE conference, Carol's car wouldn't start. "All that money for a new transmission," she said, "and now this!"

"I'd try to find the problem," Tony said, "but I'm already late. I can give you a ride."

"Then how will I get home?"

"Somebody at work, maybe?"

"Let me call Troy Hartman," Carol said.

Troy Hartman was a coworker who lived a mile away. He was always pleasant and helpful at the office, and sure enough he said he could give her a ride both ways. Tony gave her a hug and took off.

The conference was in New Hampshire, four hours away. Tony called home the first two nights and talked to both Carol and Robbie. Carol told him she had the car towed back to Atlas, but they hadn't fixed it yet.

Troy Hartman had no problem giving her rides. She made Robbie's favorite dinners the first two nights, but the third night Troy worked late so Carol called Robbie and told him she wouldn't be home for a while. He should make a cheese sandwich for supper and go to bed at nine if she wasn't back by then.

"I heard that conversation," Troy said with a smile. "I'll be done pretty soon here, I'm sorry I hung you up, what say we go over to Carter's and grab something to eat?"

Carter's was a little restaurant just around the corner. Troy insisted on paying for Carol's meal, then drove her home. It was nine thirty-five; she knew Robbie would be in bed. When Troy stopped in front of the house she said to him, "You've been such a help to me. Why don't you come inside and I'll make some coffee."

"As long as it's decaf," Troy said.

Carol made decaf and sat with him in the living room. She had him sit in Tony's chair and she sat on the couch. At dinner they'd talked about work and the people at work, but now they talked about places they wanted to visit. Troy had already been to Spain and France, and he wanted to go to the Czech Republic. Carol said, "Why?" then heard a wheezing sound upstairs and Troy said, "Is that your son?"

"He has asthma. It acts up pretty badly now and then."

"That doesn't sound good."

Carol went to the foot of the stairs and called, "Are you okay?"

The reply was weak. "Uh-huh."

She went back to the couch again. "I'll look in on him later," she said.

Robbie felt bad in the throat and chest and he got out of bed and went to his closet and took out the cane. As soon as he did, he felt somewhat better, but then a voice began: *Why did your mother bring somebody into your home when your father was gone? A man! Was that the right thing to do? It was not! Your mother is bad.*

No! Robbie thought. It's just Mr. Hartman from work, he's giving Mother rides while Daddy is gone.

It is bad, said the voice. *Very bad.*

Robbie let go of the cane; the voice faded away. But now his chest was terribly tight and he couldn't breathe. His wheezing was loud and he heard his mother on the stairs and then she was in his room. He was into his heavy-duty breather. "That's it," she said, but the wheezing continued and she took him out of his bed and guided him down the stairs.

"Troy, I hate to ask you this but we need to go to Riverside right away."

"No problem," Troy said.

Carol took Robbie's jacket from the mudroom and helped him put it on, then took the heavy socks that were in his boots and helped him put them on too. And then they were in Troy's car and Robbie continued to gasp and wheeze all the way to ER.

They examined him and treated him and his breathing settled down. On the way back home he fell asleep.

Troy carried Robbie inside and up the stairs and put him to bed.

"I can't thank you enough," Carol said.

"Anything else I can do for you?"

"Go home and get some sleep. Look what time it is!"

Troy shook his head. "The poor kid's got that damn stuff pretty bad."

"It flares up like this every so often, but yes, this one was really wicked."

"His workup is scheduled for Monday," Troy said. "Tony will be home by then, right?"

"Right," Carol said.

ROBBIE

ROBBIE WAS MUCH IMPROVED the following day. The wheezing had subsided and his chest didn't feel so tight. His father grinned when he came through the mudroom door that night. "I missed you, kid," he said. "Give me five."

"Was the conference interesting?" Robbie asked.

"So-so," his father said, and Robbie went off to the living room to watch TV.

Then Carol told Tony about the ER trip. "I should've been here," Tony said. "Maybe I shouldn't go away like that again."

"But how often does he have a really bad attack?"

"Not often, thank god. But you never know when it will strike."

"This was the worst," Carol said.

Tony entered the living room. "How you feeling now, Rob?"

"I had bad wheezing," Robbie said, still watching TV.

Tony thought that he didn't look really good, kind of washed out and tired. "I heard. Well on Monday you'll go to the doctors again and they'll fix you right up."

"I hope so."

He had put the cane in his closet and told himself he would never use it again. It hadn't helped him very much this time and told him bad things about his mother.

On Monday his father rescheduled two early appointments and took Robbie back to Riverside. He had a complete workup and they gave him a shot and a different inhaler. On the way home he said, "How come you sold Grammy's ring?"

"I needed the money, Rob."

"Because you lost a bet."

"More than one, Rob, more than one."

"I wish you wouldn't bet anymore."

"I'm not going to. Right now I'm almost free and clear and I'll try to keep it that way." As he pulled into the driveway he said, "I haven't seen your cane around."

"I put it away in my closet."

"Are you tired of it?"

"Maybe."

He didn't know what he would do with it. He hated what it had said about his mother, but he couldn't sell it or even give it away. To do that would cause bad things to happen, Grammy had said. He had to keep it. And he would—way back in his closet.

He missed another two days of school before he felt better. He watched TV with Tofu on his lap and gradually regained his strength. On Thursday his father said, "The Ramblers are in town again. Are you up for a game?"

Robbie still didn't feel like himself but the wheezing almost never came back and he wanted to go with his father. Thoughts of the man he had seen in the parking lot there that time, the man who had thrown his cane on the ground, made him nervous, but he said, "I'm fine."

"No cane this time," his father said when they got in the car to go.

"No," Robbie said.

"You're getting tired of it."

"I guess."

The Ramblers were doing very well, which was great, because Robbie was scared that his father had placed a bet. He was eating an ice cream sandwich when he asked, "Do you think that man we saw in the parking lot will be there again when the game is over?"

"No, I don't," his father said.

"I hope you're right."

"I'm definitely right. That man is dead. He died of a heart attack."

Robbie's stomach went tight. He stopped eating.

He'd had bad thoughts about that man. The cane had bitten him and he'd thrown it down on the ground. Had it made him sick? Had it given him a *heart attack*? Had it *killed* him?

"Can you finish my ice cream sandwich?" he asked his father.

"Too full, huh?" Tony said.

"Yes," Robbie said.

On the way home his father said, "That man you were

talking about. A day after we saw him, he took sick and died. Only forty-three years old."

"Uh-huh," Robbie said.

"You never know," his father said. "Bad things can happen at any time."

At home Robbie thought of the cane sitting there in his closet. It had made Buddy's dog attack, he knew it had. It had made Mr. Perkins fall off his ladder and hit his head. It had hurt the ankle of the Comets' star player. And now…it had killed a man! Had given him a heart attack!

Then he thought: *It hates my mother! Did it plan to do something bad to* her*?* If only he could get rid of it. But he couldn't, or terrible things would happen!

For the next two weeks he still didn't feel quite right. He was tired, had headaches and mild wheezing. But the really worrisome thing was he found that his mind was all mixed up. In school he had distracting thoughts, and his teacher, Ms. Hudson, reprimanded him several times for not paying attention. He kept hearing those awful voices—without even touching the cane! He even heard them in his dreams, which were usually very scary and made him jerk awake in a sweat, his heart beating hard. The same voices, over and over again! *Go away, stop, stop*! he said to himself, and prayed to God, but they kept coming back.

MRS. CARNEY

WHEN AUNT LILLIAN PICKED him up to go to church, she said, "Uncle Victor was thrilled to receive that bankbook you found. He thought he was only getting some stamps, but no. Of course, I got the bankbook *and* the house. I still don't understand why Grammy gave your father his bankbook before she died, but she had her ways."

"Uh-huh," Robbie said. Then he said, "Do you think there are any rats in Grammy's house?"

"Of course not," Lillian said. "Mother would have gotten rid of them right quick." She was quiet a moment then said, "You've had a rough time, I hear. You still don't look top notch to me."

"I feel okay. The doctors—"

"Doctors!" Lillian said. "What do they know of spirit? Now tell me honestly, how are you feeling?"

"Okay…but I hear these voices."

"Voices?" Lillian said. "What kind of voices? Grammy's voice?"

"Sometimes. But other times they're people I don't know, and sometimes they seem to be speaking a different language." He waited a couple of seconds then said, "I was in my bedroom a couple of nights ago and heard Mom and Dad talk about how they might make me go to a therapist."

"A therapist!" Lillian said. "They're even worse than doctors!" Then she frowned and said nothing the rest of the drive.

When they entered the church, she had Robbie take a seat up front, then said, "I'll be right back, I have to make a phone call."

After the service, Robbie said, "Why are we taking a different way home?

"We're going to see Mrs. Carney," Lillian said.

"What?"

"The doctors aren't making you better and you definitely need some help."

"But Mrs. Carney…"

"Are you afraid of her?"

"A little bit."

"Well don't be. She is filled with spirit."

They arrived at Mrs. Carney's home, an apartment in one of the old brick buildings on Main Street. "Now don't you fuss," Aunt Lillian said. "Mrs. Carney will help make you better."

They climbed the stairs to the second floor. By the time they reached the apartment landing Lillian was out of breath. She rang the bell.

Mrs. Carney opened the door. "We have arrived," said Lillian. "You know my nephew Robbie, don't you?"

Mrs. Carney nodded. "Welcome," she said. She was wearing the yellow turban, but not the clothing she'd worn when Robbie had seen her before. Now she was wearing a long white robe.

The apartment was very dark; there were heavy curtains over the windows and piles of boxes everywhere.

Robbie whispered to Aunt Lillian, "What's that funny smell?"

"That's incense," she replied.

Mrs. Carney led them through her small living room and into an even smaller dining room where a candle burned on the table. Robbie was surprised to see two older women sitting there.

"Gladys and Janet," Mrs. Carney said. "You know Lillian, and this is her nephew, Robbie."

The women said hello.

Gladys was black. There were only a couple of black kids in Robbie's school. They were in the upper grades and he didn't know them. But quite a few black people went to Aunt Lillian's church.

"Please sit down," Mrs. Carney said, and Robbie and Lillian did.

"Now everyone link hands."

Robbie took Aunt Lillian's hand in his; Gladys took his other hand and Janet took Aunt Lillian's free hand.

Mrs. Carney sat across from them. She had them take five deep breaths and told them to close their eyes, then she began:

"Holy spirit, I call thee forth," she said. "We beseech thee to give us aid."

She was quiet a minute and then she said, "The child you see here needs your help, and I will serve as guide."

She said some things that Robbie didn't understand—they seemed to be in a foreign language—and then she said, "Let us now be silent."

The room seemed dead, no sound at all except for the ticking of a large grandfather's clock in the shadows against the wall. Then the woman named Gladys said in a shaky voice, "I see him now. My Ralph. He looks quite well. Oh, how I miss you Ralph, I miss you so much," then she started to cry.

She cried for several minutes and Robbie felt creepy holding her hand. Then once again it was quiet. Mrs. Carney said in a soft voice, "You have touched his spirit and he has touched yours."

"Yes, yes," Gladys said, and wiped her eyes with a handkerchief.

The woman named Janet said nothing. "Janet?" Mrs. Carney said. "Can you contribute anything?"

"I hear voices," Janet said.

"Listen well," Mrs. Carney said. "They are voices of spirit."

Now Robbie was hearing them too: *Leave no don't cane make why should hold…*

It was quiet except in his head, the horrible voices in his head. Then Mrs. Carney said, "You have a talisman."

"She's talking to you," Aunt Lillian whispered.

"A magical object," Mrs. Carney said.

The cane, Robbie thought. But how did she know about that? Aunt Lillian must have told her!

"This talisman is evil," Mrs. Carney said, "and must be destroyed."

But I can't do that, Robbie thought. *I can't!* and the voices in his head became louder.

"Do you understand?" Mrs. Carney said.

"Say yes," Aunt Lillian whispered.

"Yes," Robbie said.

"Another thing," Mrs. Carney said. "You have read the old letter, and now your father should have the same test your Aunt Lillian had."

"What's that?" Robbie said.

"Aunt Lillian will explain," Mrs. Carney said. "The images are fading now, but you have your instructions. Do not fail to heed them."

"Say I won't," said Lillian, and Robbie did.

"We are finished here," Mrs. Carney said. "She rose heavily, went to a window and pulled a drape and cold gray light poured in. She returned to the table and blew out the candle. "Spirit, we thank thee for thy help," she said as candle smoke rose to the ceiling.

She led the way to the door and opened it, smiling. The two old women thanked her and went down the stairs.

When Lillian and Robbie started down Mrs. Carney said, "Remember what you must do."

"I will," Robbie said.

But out in the car again he thought: How did Mrs. Carney know about that letter? Had Grammy told her where she had hidden the box? And had she left it there for him to find? His mind was all mixed up.

"Well, that was a total surprise," Aunt Lillian said behind

the wheel. "I thought she would focus on *you*, not on your so-called talisman."

"She wants me to destroy the cane but I can't do it," Robbie said.

"Because it's so valuable," Lillian said as she pulled away. "But sometimes valuable things must be destroyed."

"It's not just that. Grammy told me that if I sold it or gave it to somebody else bad things would happen."

"She was quite sick when she told you that, Robbie. She often didn't know what she was saying. If you ask me, though, I think you should keep the cane and not harm it."

"Okay," Robbie said with a nod, "that's good. Do you think it has a spirit?"

Aunt Lillian was driving very slowly. "Spiritualists believe that everything has a spirit. Animals, trees, grass..."

"But what about things that aren't alive?"

"Well, who is to say what's alive and what isn't? Easter Islanders believe their huge stone statues hold the spirits of their dead."

"Mrs. Carney believes that the cane has a spirit," Robbie said. "If it does, can it talk?"

"I doubt that very much. You're thinking about those voices you hear?"

"Yes."

"I'm sure they don't come from the cane."

"I'm not so sure. Is its spirit evil?"

"According to Mrs. Carney, but she's not always right."

"Well, I think she's right this time. Grammy told me to learn how to use the cane and I guess I did, because bad things happened to people I thought bad thoughts about."

"Such as?"

"A kid who was bothering me. The cane bit his thumb then his dog attacked and he had to go to the hospital for stitches."

"The cane bit him?" Lillian said.

"It did."

"The Wolf's teeth are very sharp, that's why we were never allowed to touch it. But I don't believe it actually bit him or made his dog attack."

"Well, I do. And Daddy's boss. He fell off a ladder and hit his head right when he was giving Daddy a lot of trouble. Do you remember Grip?"

"Who could forget him?"

"A bird like Grip attacked the boss's head, that's why he fell."

"Grip," Lillian said. "Grammy's 'familiar' we called him."

"What's a familiar?"

"A helper. But Grip is dead."

"But a bird just like him—"

"It was a bird that *looked* like him, that's all. Probably just a common crow. They can be nasty at times."

"But maybe he has Grip's spirit."

"Nothing has anyone else's spirit, Robbie. It could have a similar spirit, but not the same one." She stopped for a light.

"And a mean man came up to Daddy in the parking lot at a hockey game and grabbed the cane away from me and it bit him, too. And the next day the man had a heart attack and died."

"Good heavens!" Lillian said. "But blaming the cane for that—"

"I'm sure it did it," Robbie said.

"Your imagination is getting the best of you," Lillian said.

They were quiet a minute, then Robbie asked, "What was that test Mrs. Carney was talking about? A test you took."

"It tells about your ancestry. I knew that I had Romanian blood, and I wanted to see if those tests could detect it, skeptic that I am. But they found it all right. Your father would have it too, of course."

The light turned green and she started off again, slow as a snail.

"But why did Mrs. Carney say he needs a test?"

"I have no idea. And I'm not sure she's right about the cane being evil, either. I'm sure you're aware that when you were two, the cane cured an illness you had."

"No. I never knew that."

"Your parents never told you?"

"No."

"Hard to believe. Well, when you were two you had a terrible illness. Your doctors had a number of tests done but came up empty. But Grammy went to your bedside with the cane and held it over you and right away you started getting better. In a couple of days, you were perfectly normal again. The cane addressed your *spirit*. The doctors didn't know about spirit, but Grammy did. So the cane has done some very good things, and that's why I wonder about Mrs. Carney's advice."

"Should Daddy take that test?"

"I doubt if he'll ever do it."

"What does he have to do?"

"Just spit in a cup, that's all. Or even just touch a cup with his lips."

"If I get a cup that he drank from and give it to you, can you get the test?"

"I can. And you know, that's a good idea, I've always had my suspicions."

"About what?"

"About his ancestry."

"But wouldn't it be the same as yours?"

"Not necessarily, there are variations. Well, here we are."

She pulled into the driveway. Robbie got out, said goodbye, and went to the door on the side of the garage.

His father always parked his car in the garage, and most of the time he threw his empty paper coffee cup in the trash can next to the door before going into the mudroom. Robbie thought: If I can get one of those cups…

He said hi to his mother, who was making lunch. His father was down in the cellar. What did Aunt Lillian mean about ancestry variations? What was she thinking?

He went upstairs to his room and changed out of his Sunday clothes. When he hung them up, he saw the cane in the back of the closet. Mrs. Carney had said it was bad and should be destroyed…

He was feeling exhausted now after the Sunday service and session at Mrs. Carney's, and he felt that his asthma might start to act up. He knew if he held the cane, it would make him feel better but he didn't want to do that. He didn't want to touch it ever again. He was almost afraid of it now, afraid it might bite, and he didn't know what to do.

ROBBIE

ON MONDAY HIS FATHER came home from work holding his empty coffee cup. As always, he threw it in the garage trash can before going into the mudroom.

Robbie retrieved it and biked to Aunt Lillian's place. She invited him in for hot cocoa, but he refused. He had to get home for dinner, he said. "Thank you for the cup," Aunt Lillian said. "I'll be very interested in the results."

On Friday, Robbie came home from sliding to find Aunt Lillian's car in their driveway. In the mudroom, as he took off his jacket and boots, he heard, "I always knew there was something different." Aunt Lillian's voice, coming from the living room.

"Those searches aren't always accurate," his father said.

Robbie went into the dining room. He wasn't sure if he should go any further.

"Oh the local ones are accurate, all right," Aunt Lillian said. "At least mine was."

"But French?" his father said.

"Believe it. Mine is Romanian, English, Belgian and Finnish, and yours is Romanian, English, Dutch and, yes, French. You definitely had a different father from Victor and me."

"I don't believe it."

"We thought you were Mother's favorite because you were the youngest, but it was more than that."

"You think *I* was her favorite?" Tony said. "So why did she leave you her house?"

"Because we shared the same religion."

"That nonsense," Tony said.

"Don't call it that!" Lillian snapped.

"How can you believe that stuff?" Tony said. "And you believe this DNA stuff too."

"I certainly do. There was this very nice man who used to stop by the house now and then and give us candy before you were born. I don't know if he sold insurance or what, but he kept showing up. Mother liked him a lot, so who knows? Come to think of it, he looked a lot like you."

"You're imagining things. As usual."

"Those tests don't lie."

Tony let out a breath. "So what happened to him?"

"He died of some kind of cancer not long after you were born. I remember Mother crying when she heard."

"And Dad never suspected anything."

"I don't think so. Of course Victor and I were just kids at the time, so how could we have suspicions?"

"Yeah." A pause, then Tony said, "A lot to think about."

"I'll give you the papers. If you want to question them,

go right ahead. If you want another test, that's up to you. But I think they're accurate. Well listen, I have to be on my way."

Another silence, then Lillian was in the dining room. "Robbie!" she said.

"Hi," Robbie said.

"How long have you been here?"

"Not long."

"Did you overhear our conversation?"

"Yes."

"So now you know why Mrs. Carney said what she did."

"You and Daddy have different fathers."

"It looks that way."

"Does it matter?"

"It matters quite a bit. We'll talk about it later." She went through the mudroom, into the garage and out the side door.

Robbie didn't know what to do. He had to go through the living room to get upstairs. He could pretend he hadn't heard what they were saying…

He entered the living room. His father was sitting in his easy chair, his head in his hands. His mother was sitting in hcr chair looking stunned.

His father looked up. "Did you hear what Aunt Lillian said?" he asked.

Robbie wanted to say he hadn't, but just couldn't do it. He nodded yes.

"We don't know if it's true," his mother said, "but these tests…"

"Aunt Lillian says it matters," Robbie said.

"Well, maybe it matters and maybe it doesn't," his father said. "But it's kind of a shock to be presented with that kind of thing." He was quiet a minute then said, "You gave Aunt Lillian one of my coffee cups."

"I did. She asked me to do it."

"Yeah. And you went with her to Mrs. Carney's."

"She made me go. I didn't want to."

"Well, that will never happen again," his father said. "And maybe going to that wacko church will stop too." He shook his head. "All these years I thought I knew who my father was, and now... Well, those tests aren't always right."

"But most of the time they are," his mother said.

It was very quiet at dinner that night. They had canned soup and crackers and watched the news, Tony and Carol barely speaking.

Robbie went up to his room, put Tofu on his lap and thought: *I have the same genes as Daddy. And his are from Grammy and the man who maybe was my real grandfather, and the rest are from Mom.*

He thought of the letter to Grammy he'd read. Had it come from Daddy's real father? Probably so. The man who sometimes came to Grammy's house with candy for the children, the man who was always smiling? The man in the letter had said he was sorry he couldn't see his child grow up. That child was Daddy! Maybe if he showed that letter to him it would help him believe the test results. But how could he ever do that?

"Tofu, I'm all mixed up," he said. "All I know is I love my Daddy no matter where he came from. And so do you."

Thoroughly worn out, with Tofu beside him, he fell asleep.

TONY

LATER, WHEN ROBBIE AND Carol were sleeping, Tony sat in the living room with the TV picture on but the sound turned down. As he smoked, he thought: Maybe that's why I drink so much, I have a genetic predisposition for it. That's no excuse, of course, but Victor and Lillian don't drink at all. The man who visited his mother, bringing candy, always smiling, was that his real father? Maybe he was always smiling because he was high all the time.

I could go for a drink right now, he thought, boy, could I go for a drink. But no, he was on the wagon and swore he wouldn't fall off.

He sat there, wondering why Lillian had taken Mrs. Carney's advice and tested his DNA. To prove that he was different from Victor and her, of course. And she had roped Robbie into it too. That wasn't right, not at all. Her and her holier than thou pretentions and she does something like this.

So the man he had always assumed was his father, the man who had died when he was eight, was *not* his father? His father was the smiling guy? He'd never met him, didn't know him at all.

But his mother had had an affair! That was the shocking part of this whole thing. Straight-laced Mother! Incredible! And she had kept that secret for the rest of her life.

He smoked another cigarette and thought about genes, the role that they played in behavior. All he knew about that kind of stuff was from TV shows, and it was confusing. Some experts felt genes were paramount and some felt environment overruled them. If the experts couldn't make up their minds, how could *he*?

He put out his cigarette, ready to go upstairs to try to sleep, when the land line rang. He picked it up.

"Tony, this is Victor."

Something was wrong; Victor never called this late. "What's up?"

"Lillian's had a stroke."

"Oh my god."

"She called me and didn't make sense, so I went over there and found her unconscious next to the phone. I called 911 and they came and took her to Riverside. They diagnosed the stroke."

"How is she now?"

"Conscious, but weak on her right side. Her speech is all messed up."

"That's terrible, Vic."

"I was afraid this might happen—might happen to *me*. Our father had a stroke at about this age. He recovered almost completely though. I don't know if you remember that."

"Our father," Tony said. "Then Lillian didn't tell you."

"Tell me what?"

"That we had different fathers."

"What?"

"She had a DNA test done on my saliva. It shows we came from different backgrounds."

A pause on the line. "You had her do a DNA test? Why?"

"I had nothing to do with it. She got Robbie to give her a cup I used and she sent in a sample."

"But why in the world…"

"Mrs. Carney," Tony said. "She recommended it and Lillian always does what she says."

"That fraud!" Victor said.

"Well, fraud or not, Lillian had it done and it turns out we have different genetic histories. She was probably calling you to tell you this when she had the stroke. She probably wanted *you* to test your DNA and compare it to hers."

"This is hard to believe."

"Well, believe it. It means you and Lil are my half-siblings."

The line was silent again then Victor said, "I always wondered. After Lil was born eight years went by without another child. My father had had his stroke by then and we figured he wasn't up to having more kids. Then suddenly you came along. It was shocking to Lil and me, it really was. We resented you, all the attention you got for being the baby of the family."

"And I felt it," Tony said, "especially from Lil."

"This whole thing is amazing," Victor said.

"And Dad…your father never suspected?"

"I don't know. *We* certainly never suspected. You were more of an athlete than either of us but we figured that was just the roll of the dice. After you were born that salesman or whatever he was only showed up a couple of times."

"Lillian says he died of cancer. She remembers Mother crying when she heard."

"We never even knew his name."

Tony shook his head. "My father—*your* father—died when I was eight. I never knew my real father—whoever he was—at all. But what does it matter? What's past is past. From the age of eight all I knew was my mother. And I never knew *this* about her."

"She had an affair—while our father was still alive!" Victor said. "Incredible."

"Sure is."

"There were plenty of things she didn't tell us, but this takes the cake. Ruth will be shocked."

"Carol already knows, of course. But back to Lil. Can she speak? What do the doctors say?"

"She's hard to understand," Victor said. "And she seems angry."

"That doesn't surprise me. But they think she'll recover?"

"They do. But if I remember Father, she'll never be quite the same."

"I'll go see her tomorrow," Tony said.

"I may be there too," Victor said. "We're all she has."

"Except for Mrs. Carney," Tony said.

In the morning Tony told Carol about the call and Robbie was there. "What's a stroke?" he asked.

"Something bad happens in your brain," Tony said. "It

can affect your movement and your speech."

"Oh," Robbie said, and thought: *the cane had nothing to do with this, I never even took it out of the closet. And Aunt Lillian told me not to destroy it, so why should it attack her? It might even want to help her.* "When are we going to see her?" he asked.

"As soon as we finish breakfast," his father said.

ROBBIE

ROBBIE INSISTED ON TAKING the cane. "I really need to take it, I need to, it might help Aunt Lillian."

"How would it ever do that?" his mother said.

"I don't know," Robbie said, "but it might."

On the ride to Riverside thoughts filled his head. They were not his thoughts but they were good.

Lillian was on the hospital's ground floor. A nurse told Robbie that he could show her his cane.

She looked very different to him: thin and pale and very tired. Everyone said hello and she tried to answer but everything came out distorted and wrong. She looked very upset and then she began to cry.

"Don't cry," Robbie said. "Please don't," and he held the cane above her and closed his eyes.

"Robbie, what are you doing?" his mother asked, but he didn't answer. He just kept holding the cane above his aunt.

And soon she stopped crying. "I feel a bit better," she said—and it came out right.

"You're going to be fine," Tony said. "I can feel it."

To this, Aunt Lillian said, "Mother's cane. Robbie, you

have learned…an excellent way…to use it."

They spent another half hour there. Lillian was quite worn out by then. Tony promised to come back tomorrow and they left.

Out in the car again, he said, "Well maybe that cane is magical and maybe not, but it sure seemed to help."

"It did," Robbie said. "I know it did."

When he got home, he went to his room and put the cane back in his closet. It doesn't just do bad things, he thought, it does good things too. Aunt Lillian will get well, I know she will—because of the Wolf!

ROBBIE

———— ✳ ————

ROBBIE WENT BACK TO the hospital with his father the following day, Sunday, and Lillian had made remarkable gains. Her speech was much clearer and she was smiling. "Almost felt well enough to go to church this morning," she said, "thanks to Mother's cane. Just think if we'd destroyed it, as Mrs. Carney asked us to. Where would I be now?"

"She asked you to destroy the cane?" Tony said.

"She did," Robbie said. He was holding it tight and felt a soft buzzing.

"It has filled me with spirit," Lillian said. "Bless you, Robbie." She frowned. "Where is Carol this morning?"

"She had some important things to do," Tony said.

"Mmm," Lillian said, then smiled at Robbie again. "If I'm not well enough to go church next Sunday," she said, "maybe your father will take you."

To this, Tony said, "You'll probably be all better by then."

"I certainly hope so," Lillian said. "I really do depend on those services."

On the way home, Robbie asked, "Do you believe in what Aunt Lillian believes?"

"Like what, Rob? There are spirits in everything? Trees and stuff?"

"Yes, and that the cane has a spirit too and it can heal?"

"I don't know what to believe anymore, but I think that cane stuff is all in her head."

"But she was so much better today."

"Spontaneous recovery," Tony said. "It happens all the time."

ROBBIE

BY THE END OF the week, Lillian was sent back home, and Robbie went to visit her.

"I know the cane helped," she said. "It helped a lot."

"Mrs. Carney said—"

"I know what she said, but that was before it helped me get better. She was here this morning and we talked about it. We agreed that the cane can cause bad things but good things too." She smiled. "You're enjoying the figurines?"

"Oh yes," he said, but the truth was he'd put them away in the bottom drawer of his bureau. He didn't want to play with them anymore. They reminded him of Grammy's house—and the Wolf, which had made him tell so many lies!

"We were never allowed to touch them when we were kids," Aunt Lillian said. "Mother was afraid we might harm them, they're so old. I'm glad she let you play—" She frowned. "Now there's that tapping sound again."

She turned to the window. "That bird!" she said. "It looks so much like Grip! What does it want from me?"

"It taps on my window too," Robbie said.

"It does? The same bird?"

"I think so."

"Well at least Grip could talk. It could tell you it wanted suet. Who knows what this one wants?"

"Grip used to say 'murder.'"

Aunt Lillian laughed. "Yes, it did. Now look, next week I ought to be able to go to church again. I'll come by and pick you up."

"Okay," Robbie said. Then he said, "That thing that you told my father before you got sick—that he had a different father than you and Uncle Victor have. I think it's worrying him. He doesn't seem happy."

"Just being honest," Aunt Lillian said. "We must know the truth at all costs."

"But maybe that test was wrong," Robbie said.

"I doubt that very much," Aunt Lillian said.

Robbie knew that the test was right, but he wasn't sure that his father believed it. He thought of the letter in the box he had found in Grammy's cellar. *The man who wrote that letter must be my father's real father!* he thought. If his father saw that letter, he would believe that the DNA test was right.

He rode his bike to Brett's. In his room he asked to see the box, and Brett got it out of his closet.

"I need to borrow that letter, the one from that man," he said.

"How come?"

"I just need to."

As Brett opened the box, they both heard a tapping sound at the window and turned to look.

"That bird again," Brett said.

"It taps on my window too."

"The same bird?"

"It looks the same.

"The one we saw at your grandmother's house, the crow."

"Not a crow, a raven. But tell me. Do you hear any voices in your head?"

"Voices? You mean like people talking?"

"Yes."

"No, just the tapping. It's driving me crazy. I chase it away but it comes right back. I have to wear earplugs at night 'cause it taps then too. What does it want from us?"

"I don't know. Maybe the letter."

Brett took it out of the box and gave it to him.

"Good," Robbie said. "The bird will probably fly back to my house now."

"I hope it does," Brett said. "But I still have the box."

"Amazing," his father said. They had just finished dinner. He was still at the table, drinking coffee. "Where did you find it?"

"Where I found the ring," Robbie said. "Way in the back of the drawer."

"Why didn't you show it to me when you found the ring?"

"I forgot."

His father squinted. "Mmm," he said. "I guess we ought to pull that drawer out of there and see what else we can find.

Well, this pretty much clinches it. This guy was my birth father."

"Who was he?" Carol asked.

"No names are mentioned," Tony said. "It sounds like he thinks he's dying—and maybe he did."

"Your mother's husband, Roger, never knew that you weren't his child."

"Right."

"You believe the DNA test now."

"I do." He got up from the table, went to the sideboard and, to Carol's great dismay, he filled a small glass with bourbon and drank it down.

In his room, Robbie said to Tofu: "I did the right thing. Now Daddy believes the test. But he's very upset that he didn't have the same father as Aunt Lillian and Uncle Victor, and what can I do about that? He'll just have to get used to it, I guess. But he's starting to drink again!

The tapping at the window started then. It was dark out and he couldn't see the bird. "Go away, go away, go away!" he said, and Tofu made an angry sound deep in her throat.

ROBBIE

WHEN HE SAW BRETT at school, Brett told him the bird was back.

"But why?" Robbie said. "I thought I did what it wanted me to. What does it want from you?"

"The box, I guess."

"But why?"

"I don't know, but its tapping just won't stop!"

"Maybe it wants me to give the box to my father. There are all those papers in it and maybe some are worth money. I could say that I found it in Grammy's garage, but he doesn't want me to go over there by myself."

"That tapping!" Brett said.

It was a terrible week. His father was drunk every day when he came home late from work—he had been to the Rusty Bucket—and argued with his mother. "Whose *spirit* does Mother commune with now?" he said. "The spirit of the man I *thought* was my father or my *real* father?" There was a shouting match about a gambling debt. "Again!" his mother said. "You've done it again and I won't help you out this time! I *can't* help you out this time! And don't expect Victor to help you out either!" She slammed her fist on the table, broke into tears and ran upstairs.

Robbie wanted to use the cane to help but what could it do? The DNA test was accurate, no doubt about that anymore, and the cane couldn't do a thing about it. Could the cane keep his father from getting drunk? Robbie had tried to use it that way before but it hadn't worked. So most nights he went to his room with Tofu and searched his computer for answers and just became more and more confused.

There was only one good thing: the bird had apparently gone away. He never heard it tapping anymore and never saw it outside. Maybe it finally understood that it had completed its work—Grammy's work!—and wasn't needed anymore.

"I killed it," Brett said.

They were on the school playground. Kids were running all over the place.

"You *what?*" Robbie said.

"I couldn't stand it anymore," Brett said. "Putting those earplugs in every night. So I went outside and waited until it lit on the maple tree next to my window, then got real close and shot it. The arrow went right through its body. It let out a terrible cry and fell onto the snow. I went inside to get a rag to wipe my hands off when I pulled the arrow out, but when I came out again the bird was gone."

"How could that happen?" Robbie said.

"The arrow was lying on the snow, without any blood on it, but the bird wasn't there."

"A cat took it away. Or maybe a fisher."

"But how could they get the arrow out?" Brett said. "And there wasn't any blood on it, the raven had to bleed."

"Maybe not," Robbie said. "Maybe it was a magical bird."

"What do you mean?"

"Its spirit was magical."

"And its body just…vanished?"

"Maybe so."

"That's really spooky," Brett said.

"I sure wish you hadn't killed it; you didn't have to, its work was done."

"Then why did it come back here?"

"I don't know," Robbie said. "Maybe it got mixed up."

Brett wasn't in school the next day. The teacher said he was sick. He wasn't there the next day, either, so Robbie biked to his house after school.

Brett's mother opened the door with a worried look. "He's very sick," she said. "I don't think you should see him today."

"Just for a minute or two," Robbie said.

"I don't want you to catch what he has."

"I'm sure I won't."

"Just for a minute, then."

He was lying in bed and his skin was pale. "I'm so tired," he said.

"What is it? What's wrong?"

"The doctor thinks it's some kind of flu. I went to him this morning. But you know what I think? I think I shouldn't have killed that bird, that's when I started feeling bad."

"I hope that's not what made you sick."

"I think it was."

"If it was, I can probably help. I can use the Wolf."

"But the Wolf and the bird...they were together."

"Maybe, maybe not. Anyway, I can give it a try. I'll go get it and come right back."

Robbie biked home again and ran up to his room.

After he'd used the cane to help Aunt Lillian, he'd put it way back in his closet again so he wouldn't see it. He still didn't trust it to do what he wanted.

He opened the closet door and looked inside, looked all around.

And the cane was gone.

Gone! How could it be gone?

Then he thought: His father. His father had sold it to pay off his gambling debt!

His father had just come home, he could hear the car. He ran down the stairs, through the kitchen and into the mudroom. "Daddy!" he said. "My cane is gone!"

Tony hung up his coat. He smelled of alcohol. He simply shrugged.

"It was mine!" Robbie said. "It didn't belong to you, it was mine! Grammy gave it to *me*!"

"I thought you were tired of it," his father said, stepping into the kitchen.

"No! No! And now I need it real bad, and you took it, didn't you? You took it and sold it!"

His father shook his head. "Not sold," he said. "Pawned. You can get it back if you have the money. Unless someone else has bought it."

"I need it!" Robbie said. "Brett's sick and I need it to make him well."

"I'm sure Brett will get well without it," his father said.

"No! He won't! It isn't a regular illness, it's something else that only the cane can fix! The way it fixed Aunt Lillian!"

"You really believe the cane did that?"

"I do!"

Just then Carol came into the kitchen. "What's all the shouting about?" she said.

"Dad took my cane!" Robbie said. "And Brett has an illness that only the cane can fix!"

"What? Tony, what have you done?"

"Okay, listen, I had a deadline, I needed the money, I pawned the cane. We can still get it back. I mean who would ever want such an ugly thing?"

"My god," Carol said. "It was Robbie's, and you didn't even ask him!"

"I figured I have a big sale coming up in a couple of days and after that I'll have the money to get it back."

"You figured. You're always figuring. Things will always work out, won't they?"

"Mom, I really need it," Robbie said. "Brett killed the bird and now he's really sick."

"He killed the bird?"

"The black one that kept tapping at my window. The raven that looked like Grip."

"Good riddance," Tony said, flopping down at the kitchen table.

"I don't have the money," Carol said, "but we have to get it somewhere. I hate that cane but we need to get it back." She thought for a minute then said, "We're going to Victor's."

"We are?" Tony said.

"Not you, you're worthless."

"Worthless," Tony said. "You know, you're right. I just don't feel like *me* anymore."

"What?"

"You know who your father was and I don't."

"Big deal! There are millions of adopted children who don't know who their fathers—or their mothers—are, and they're doing just fine, that's no excuse."

"But that's different," Tony said. "Most of them never knew… I thought that Lillian and Victor… See, they're only half…"

"Put your coat on, Robbie, we're going to Uncle Victor's. Hurry up, we don't have any time to lose. Where's the pawn ticket, Tony?"

"Upstairs…in my study, top desk drawer."

CAROL

VICTOR WAS SHOCKED THAT Tony had pawned the cane. But he signed a blank check to the pawn shop, and Carol hurried there with Robbie.

When they came through the pawn shop door Robbie was startled to see that a man was holding the Wolf. He was dressed in a suit and tie, had rosy cheeks and white hair. "So how much do you want for it?" he asked the clerk behind the counter.

The clerk gave a figure that Robbie couldn't hear.

"Too much," said the customer, shaking his head.

Robbie ran over to him. "You don't want that cane," he said.

"What?" the man laughed. "And who are you?"

"That cane is mine. I have a ticket for it."

"Oh you do."

"Mom! Show the man the ticket."

"Carol reached into her purse and brought it out."

"So you pawned it," the white-haired man said.

"My husband did."

"Uh-huh. And now you want it back."

"It will bite you," Robbie said.

"Quite an imagination," said the man with a grin. Then suddenly his expression changed to one of shock. He looked at the hand that was holding the cane and it was bleeding. "What the hell? How…? Here, take it!" he said, and thrust it at Robbie, who grabbed it. "How did that happen?"

"The cane doesn't like you."

"No, I can't understand..." To the clerk: "Did you see it bite?"

"I don't think it bit," said the clerk, "I think you caught your hand on one of its teeth."

"Like hell! It bit me! What is it with that thing?"

"I really don't know, sir."

"Well forget it!" the man said, and stormed out the door.

Carol wrote a check for the pawn amount plus a fee, and handed it to the clerk along with the ticket.

"Craziest thing I ever saw," said the clerk. "The guy actually thought it bit him!"

"It did," Robbie said. "Now we have to go to Brett's."

Brett's parents were startled to see them. Carol tried to explain, but Robbie just ran upstairs with the cane and into Brett's room.

Brett was asleep. Robbie held the cane above him and squeezed it tight and thought, *Get well, get well, get well. Brett didn't know about spirits in birds, you've made a mistake, he thought he was killing a regular crow, not a magical one. Please help him get well, oh please! He's my very best friend!*

He waited, heard his mother's voice downstairs, and then Brett's eyes came open. "Robbie," he said. "What are you doing here?"

"You're going to be okay," Robbie said.

Brett looked confused. "I am? But how do you know?"

"The cane told me so."

"The Golden Wolf," Brett said, his eyes on the cane.

"That's right. You'll feel much better soon."

"I hope so, Rob."

"You will. But please don't kill more birds, please don't kill *anything*."

Downstairs he said, "He's already feeling better."

Brett's mother raised her eyebrows. "He is? I'm going right up."

Mr. Weston said, "I sure hope you're right. It was good of you to come see him."

"He's my very best friend," Robbie said.

On the drive back home his mother said, "I always thought what Grammy told you about that cane was nonsense, but now I wonder."

"It isn't nonsense," Robbie said. The cane was warm in his hands.

"Maybe you can use it on your father," his mother said. "He needs help, he really does."

It was terrible to think that his father needed help. His father was good, he was strong, he worked hard, he could do anything. He built most of their house by himself! But the cane hadn't helped him stop drinking...

"Mom?" he said.

"What, Rob?"

"I have something to tell you."

She was looking straight ahead through the windshield. "Yes?"

"I lied to you and Dad."

"Oh? About what?"

"I went to Grammy's house three times without telling you. That's how I found the will and Dad's bankbook and Grammy's ring and that letter."

His mother was quiet a minute then said, "I noticed one time that the key to her house was missing but thought your father took it. But instead *you* took it."

"I did."

"And I wondered about what you told us, especially about the letter. Why didn't you tell us you were going there?"

"I was scared you wouldn't let me, but I knew it was important. The Wolf told me it was. I took it every time and it helped me find those things."

"It did. You're sure of that."

"Well, yes."

His mother shook her head. "Well, whatever, those things *were* important. I can't say I approve of your methods but I sure can't quarrel with the results."

At home as he mounted the stairs his thoughts were terribly confused. He put the cane back in his closet again, way in the back, but the worrisome thoughts continued. *Your mother is bad wants your father stop drinking when it is his only comfort...*

On his bed he held Tofu and said, "My mother is *not* bad, she's good, she's good and wants to help my father any way she can. Stop saying those things!"

But who was saying them? The cane? Or were they *his* thoughts? He pressed his hands over his ears and said, "Stop! Stop! Mother is good, she is *good*! Oh Tofu, what can I do?"

JEFF

JEFF WAS STUCK, AND what could he do?

Whenever that happened, he needed a change. In town he had multiple options but here there was nothing to do except read different stuff and mull things over and go for walks.

The river was completely frozen now but he didn't risk going out on it.

He had more migraines, and Richard had come back twice. Each time, his complexion was pale and he seemed to have less energy. His head and shoulders sparkled like mad and he wouldn't stay long, but he kept urging Jeff to try a new path until Jeff finally said, "I don't know if I'm capable of it. Maybe I just can't do what you want me to."

"I'm sure you can," Richard said, "or I wouldn't persist."

So maybe the way to banish Richard for good was to do what he wanted—try something different.

On his way back from one of his walks he thought of a story idea he'd had a while ago and what Richard had said: "Why don't you try something small? A short story. Real short."

Okay, Jeff thought, he would try something small. If he

failed at that, he'd forget about anything more than what he was already doing. Maybe Richard would leave him alone after that. And who knew, maybe a different kind of story would rev up his engine and get him back on track with his book.

So he wrote a draft, reworked it again and again, and finally, after a couple of days—which he enjoyed, he had to admit—came up with:

"A Half-Finished Bridge"

"Magnificent!" Lucinda said as she entered the mammoth kitchen.

Hillary smiled broadly, her teeth suspiciously white for a woman approaching fifty. "I said to Peter, look, while we're doing it, let's just really *do* it."

The place had been finished a month ago, and this was Hillary's combination Christmas party/open house.

"These countertops," Lucinda said as she turned to her husband. "Aren't they wonderful, David?"

"Wonderful," David said.

They were granite, and made him think of deli mustard: dull yellow with small brown flecks. Given the size of the room, they had to have cost a mint. A central island big enough for a child to skate on was also topped with the stuff.

"Durable, natural, and ever so easy to clean," said Hillary.

David nodded, then looked at the floors, and Hillary said, "They're a new Swedish laminate, practically indestructible."

"I thought they were real wood at first."

"Everyone does. The technology nowadays is amazing."

Other people came into the kitchen, and David and Lucinda left. In the dining room Lucinda said, "What a beautiful house."

"You think so?"

"Don't you?"

"It's just like a million other houses, like out of a magazine. It has no character, there's nothing distinctive about it."

"Well, *I* think it's beautiful," Lucinda said. And the *space.* Our whole downstairs would fit in that kitchen."

"Our whole damn *house* would fit in that kitchen. That fridge is the size of Mount Rainier, and that stove—six burners, two ovens..."

"Isn't it great?"

David shrugged. "Do they cook a lot?"

"I don't think they cook at all, they eat out most nights."

"So what's the point?"

"It's just nice to have a big kitchen."

"Why?"

"Look, David, don't be difficult, okay? Let's just have a good time."

"I'm having a wonderful time," David said. "A terrific time."

The house was filling up. People went to the kitchen and poured themselves drinks, then went to the dining room, piled small plates full of cheeses, barbecued wings and slices of ham and talked and talked above background music, lighthearted jazz. David got drinks for himself and Lucinda.

Lucinda chatted with friends from work, and David wandered around.

The fireplace in the living room was covered with rough tan "stone" that had never seen a quarry, as the kitchen floor had never seen a forest. The "stone" had also come from Sweden? The hearth must have come from Saturn; David had never seen that shade of green before on the planet earth. The beams of the cathedral ceiling, high above in the stratosphere, were the color of clover honey. The room was the kind of place that would never be used except on occasions like this.

The family room had off-white walls, a Van Gogh sunflower print and a huge home theater. Some men that David didn't know were watching a football game. He watched for a bit though he had no interest in football games, then left his empty glass at the bar, which was granite of course, but black, not mustard-colored. He wondered how much granite was left in the world.

He went upstairs. The banister's rail was gleaming oak. In the hallway he stopped at a mirror: oval, framed in gold. Last week he'd turned forty-five, but the mirror made him look older. Made him look *old*. He stared at himself, at the pouches below his eyes and the gray at his temples. Maybe it's not the mirror, he thought, maybe this is how I really look. Would Hillary Peckham, who bleached her teeth and colored her hair, keep a mirror that added years?

He glanced at the bedrooms, their walls of closets, the baths with their gold-fixtured spas and acres of tile—and granite countertops, this time gray. He came to a study with built-in bookshelves, a desk with computer and fax-printer-scanner combo, and furniture covered in fabric that looked like silk. Feeling drained, he entered the room and sat on the golden couch. Real silk, it had to be...

Then he suddenly thought: What's *wrong* with me? What's the difference how big this house is, what the goddamn countertops are made of? The Peckhams are decent people, *good* people—

He let out a breath and looked at the walls, at the books on the shelves. A few biographies and mysteries, but most of the stuff dealt with business—management and marketing. He thought of the book he was editing, a history of trade in the Civil War. A mind-numbing task. Well, tomorrow he ought to be finished with it.

"Hi."

He turned to the doorway to see a child, a girl of maybe five. She had short blond hair, a pale narrow face, and remarkable eyes: gray irises rimmed with black. David was instantly struck by the feeling he'd met her before somewhere, a long time ago. It unnerved him. "Hi," he said.

The girl crossed the threshold. "Why are you sitting in here?" she asked.

"Just taking a break from the party," David said.

"Don't you like parties?"

"I like them okay."

"Are you a poet?"

This made him smile. "Did somebody tell you that I was a poet?"

"My mommy did. So *are* you?"

"Not really. I've written some poems, but what I really am is a copy editor."

"What's that?"

"That's someone who reads things before they're printed. You know what printed is?"

"That's a printer right there," she said with a nod at the combo.

"Right. Well, before books are printed, somebody reads them and makes sure they don't have mistakes. That's what I do."

"That's good," the girl said. "Do you do that with poetry books?"

"Sometimes."

The girl nodded gravely and said, "Well I know a poem, you want to hear it?"

"You bet, I'm all ears."

The girl frowned. "No you're not."

David smiled again. "That's just an expression. It means that I really do want to hear it."

"Oh," said the child. Then, training her clear gray eyes on his, she said in a steady voice, "'First snow falling on a half-finished bridge.' Basho, Japan, seventeenth century."

"That's amazing," David said.

"It's snowing," the child said.

David went to the window and twisted the wand on the blinds. A spotlight was shining through thick white whirling flakes. There had been a few flurries a couple of weeks ago, but this was the first real storm. It had not been predicted. David didn't know this area well, he'd had trouble finding this street, and he thought of the long ride home. "It sure *is* snowing," he said, "it's a blizzard."

He turned to the room again and the child was gone. He went downstairs, but didn't see her anywhere.

In the dining room, where the talk was loud and the music faint, Lucinda was with more people David didn't know. She was holding a green plastic plate that had fruitcake on it. "Well, here you are," she said with a smile, and introduced him to everyone.

"It's really snowing out," he said. "We probably shouldn't stay much longer."

"It's snowing?" the man he had just shaken hands with said.

"It's really coming down."

"I hate to leave," Lucinda said. "It seems like we just got here."

"I know, but it's really bad."

The car had three inches of snow on the windshield. David had gloves on and brushed it off, brushed the snow off the roof and the other windows. Cold flakes melted on his cheeks.

Inside, with the heater blasting tepidly, he wiped his face with a tissue. Switching the lights and wipers on he started out, just creeping along.

He left the development, turning right. There weren't any houses here, just trees. No street lights. Lucinda said, "So you were your usual sociable self again."

"Well, what do you want me to do?" David said. "I don't know those people. You work with them, I don't."

"You could make an attempt."

"An attempt to what? Talk to them about my thrilling profession?"

"Yes. About anything."

"I didn't see *them* making any attempts to talk to *me*," David said. He stared at the furious snow and said, "Did you tell Hillary I was a poet?"

"No," Lucinda said. "At least not recently. Maybe a while ago. Did she ask you if you were a poet?"

"She didn't ask me anything. All we talked about was her goddamn kitchen."

"I love those countertops."

"Okay, so the Peckhams have money."

"I'm not—"

"Our house will never appear in a magazine."

"I don't mean that."

"So fancy, so luxurious. And they don't even cook, it doesn't make any sense, it's pure ostentation."

Lucinda rolled her eyes. She was quiet a couple of minutes then said, "I sure wish I had that space."

"You don't do that much cooking either," David said. "And I do none at all."

Lucinda's sigh meant: enough, already. "So where did you get to?" she asked.

"I went upstairs to check things out. I thought I might find at least *something* of interest, but no such luck. I sat on a couch in the study up there, and the next thing I knew, this girl came in, she's maybe five, blond hair—"

"Their change-of-life baby," Lucinda said. "And she's certainly changed *their* lives. Wow, just imagine, at our age..."

"I can't," David said. Their only child, Jon, was twenty-two, and David wondered: would having a five-year-old make you feel younger—or wear you out quicker? Maybe both. "God, everything's speeding up so much," he said. "It's going so *fast*."

"Except you."

"It's the best I can do in this snow," David said. "I can just about see." He leaned forward; it didn't help. "So anyway, this kid—"

"Her name is Ariel."

"That's nice, she didn't tell me that. An airy spirit."

"What?"

"The sprite in *The Tempest*—Ariel."

"I'm not familiar with that play."

"It's one of my favorites. Anyway, she asked me if I was a poet, she said that her mother had told her I was. I denied it—"

"Why?" Lucinda interrupted. "You *are* a poet."

"Come on, how long has it been since I've written a poem?"

"You've had things published."

"Ancient history. So Ariel says she knows a poem and then she recites it—a poem by Basho, if you can believe it. 'First snow falling on a half-finished bridge.' Imagine, this little kid saying that."

Lucinda sniffed a laugh. "I read it in the powder room, it was on the calendar there. She probably said it to everybody."

"Maybe," David said, and now he was frowning.

"Whatever, she said it to *me*." He thought of the child's piercing eyes.

"So is that a great poem?" Lucinda said. "Or even a poem at all? It seems so...nothing."

"It's not," David said, "it's really *something*. Think about it. The bridge is only half-finished, and winter's coming. Construction will get more difficult. Maybe it will have to stop. Maybe the bridge will *never* be finished."

"Uh-huh."

"Or look at it this way. The poet is aging, there's white in his hair. He has all these projects he wants to do, and he's growing old. He's afraid he'll never complete his life's work."

"How do you get all that out of those few words?"

"Well doesn't it make sense?"

"I guess."

David stared through the windshield. The snow was coming straight at him, thick and fast. He remembered his face in the mirror and said, "There were so many things that I wanted to do."

"So do them," Lucinda said, "nobody's stopping you."

David was gripping the steering wheel tightly. "Nobody at all," he said, squinting hard at the snow.

"What road are we on?" Lucinda asked. "Do you know where you're going?"

David didn't reply to this.

As the migraine faded away this time the shimmering was barely visible and Richard was lost in its shadows. His voice was almost inaudible as he said, "Congratulations, you're on the right track, you're addressing your current concerns. You're ready to go to the book you gave up on, the one about the poet, and I think you'll be surprised. As for me, I'm quite feeble, just look—I have no hands, my entire right arm is going…"

Jeff said, "I didn't mean for you—"

"You've written my story—and of course it was *your* story all along. You've heard all I have to say, and I wish you the best of luck."

Jeff said, "I might need some help—"

Richard's lips continued to move but no words came out and then, just like that, he was gone.

Gone for good. For *good.* Oddly enough, Jeff was going to miss him. How about that?

In his sleep that night, the road ahead came in a dream—a beautiful, calm and useful one—and he woke up ready to go.

ROBBIE

BRETT WAS IN SCHOOL the following week but still wasn't quite right, sad-looking and pale. Robbie was glad he was back but worried for him and also for himself. Every so often his thoughts went wrong again, bad thoughts about his mother. *It's the Wolf again,* he kept telling himself. *It's not really me, it's the Wolf.*

One night his mother went out to a meeting. He was sitting alone with his father in the living room watching TV, a comedy show, when the land line rang. His father put down his drink, set his cigarette in the ashtray, lifted the receiver and said hello.

"What?" he said. "Where? My god! Okay, yes, I'll be right there!"

He jumped up and rushed to the mudroom and put on his coat.

Robbie followed him there and said, "What happened? What's wrong?"

"Your mother was driving home when she slid on a patch

of ice and hit a utility pole and got hurt. She's in Riverside, that's where I'm going."

"I want to come too."

"No, you stay here."

"But—"

"Stay here and tend the fire," his father said. He hurried into the garage and started his car.

Robbie just stood there, stunned, as his father pulled away and the garage door closed. He slowly went back to the living room. The TV still babbled on and he turned it off.

An accident! Mother! Then he started to wonder: Had the Wolf done that? Put ice on the road, made her lose control? Of course not, the cane was in his bedroom closet. But it hated his mother...

He sat on the couch and burst into tears and Tofu came over and sat in his lap. "Oh Tofu," he said, "Please let her be okay. Please, please." And then he said a prayer.

An agonizing hour of worry and fear that he'd done something wrong, something to hurt his mother, his stomach tight, his lungs heavy. Then the land line rang.

He picked it up. His father.

"Mom is pretty confused and in some pain, but her vital signs are good. Her leg's been hurt and she has something wrong with her stomach. I'm going to stay here for now. Just keep the fire going and I'll call you again."

Robbie's heart started racing. He sniffed his fingers. "Is she going to die?" he asked.

"No, no, she'll be all right, she's just banged up."

"Will she come home tonight?"

"No, she needs to stay here a while. She needs the doctors."

"Oh. Well say hi for me."

"I already have. She's been asking for you."

"Can I talk to her?"

"I'm afraid not, Rob; she's sleeping now."

When he got off the phone, he put more wood on the fire and sat there again with his thoughts. And other mixed-in thoughts, cane thoughts. "*Stop, stop!*" he said.

He knew that the cane could make his mother better. It had made Aunt Lillian better after her stroke. The doctors had been amazed by how quickly she recovered. But Aunt Lillian liked the cane because it was Grammy's and his mother hated it. And it hated her too.

"Rob?"

He had fallen asleep on the couch. Confused, he saw his father standing over him. Then it all came back and he groggily asked, "How's Mom?"

"She was still asleep when I left."

"But she's all right?"

"She's hurt, but not too bad. Let's go to bed."

"Okay. Come on, Tofu."

He went upstairs and lay on the bed and thought: *Wolf, I know you don't like my mother, but please, help her out this time. If you do that now, I won't ever ask for more favors.*

Then his thoughts went tangled and strange and he slept, but not well.

The next day his father went to Riverside first thing, and Robbie went to school. He was terribly tired, had stomach pains, and had no appetite at lunch. "Did your mother get hurt real bad?" Brett asked. He still didn't look quite right.

"Pretty bad," Robbie said. "But not real bad."

"But she's still in Riverside."

"She hurt her leg. And maybe her stomach too."

He fell asleep at his desk in the afternoon, but Brett, who sat beside him, poked him awake.

His father was there when he got back home. "Mom wants to see you," he said, "so let's go."

"I need the cane," Robbie said.

"Maybe they won't let you take it in," his father said.

"But the hospital let me take it in when Aunt Lillian was sick."

"True," his father said.

"And other people have canes."

"True again."

They let him take it in.

His mother, like Aunt Lillian, looked different, washed out and somehow lost. When she saw the cane, her eyes opened wide and she said, "What did you bring that for?"

"I thought it might help you," Robbie said.

But he knew that wasn't true. On the ride to Riverside the voice kept saying over and over again that his mother was bad, so bad, and he fought it with all his might. My father loves her! he said again and again in his head. He loves her! And you like my father and should help! But the voice kept telling him she was bad.

He held the cane tightly and closed his eyes and wished with all his heart for his mother to get better, but the cane didn't buzz at all, it seemed totally dead. "Take that awful thing away," she said. "It's making me feel worse."

"I guess we should go now," Robbie said as the voice in his head said, *bad.*

"I want to stay just a little bit longer," his father said. "You go wait in the car."

His mother had to stay in Riverside another few days for various tests. During that time his father had nothing to drink and even seemed to be cutting back on his smoking.

But Robbie was not feeling well. He was always tired, had little appetite and stomach pains. His asthma had started up again and he had to use his breather a lot.

"I think the cane doesn't like me anymore because I tried to help my mother with it," he told Brett.

"It's full of bad magic, like Mrs. Carney said."

"Both bad and good. After all, it helped you."

"It did. I felt so terrible after I killed that bird, but then you came and used the cane. But I still don't feel like I used to. It's like it helped me a little but not all the way."

"It won't help my mother at all," Robbie said. "My Grammy didn't like her and set the cane against her. And now it doesn't even like *me* anymore. And probably doesn't like my father, either. He pawned it! It's just lucky we got it back."

"You should have left it at the pawn shop, I guess," Brett said, "and hoped that somebody bought it."

"Somebody almost did," Robbie said. "But Grammy said if I lost it or sold it or gave it to someone, bad things would happen."

"They're already happening," Brett said.

When his mother came home, he tried to do things for her but had no energy. Her leg was wrapped up and she had trouble getting around, but the worst of it was she was always tired, just like him. And her stomach still hurt, just like his.

Robbie was sure that the cane was doing all this. He would hold it and say, "Help us, help us," but the voice in his head would just say that his mother was bad. And he prayed every day, at least once.

Then he started to hear the voice when he wasn't holding the cane, when it was still in the closet. "Stop!" he would say, but the voice wouldn't quit. Most nights he could hardly sleep and in school he was exhausted, in a daze. He couldn't go to Brett's because he didn't feel well enough, and after he did his homework, he'd fall asleep.

TONY

TONY WAS BESIDE HIMSELF. He'd quit drinking so he could concentrate on Carol but there were times when he wanted the booze so bad.

Carol was not getting better. She should have improved by now but every day was the same for her or even a little worse. She had no appetite, was always exhausted, and slept most of the day. The doctors had changed her meds several times but nothing seemed to work.

The doctors said she should go back into Riverside for another workup and she said no, she didn't want that, she was sure she would soon improve. But Tony, who made the meals (most of them frozen supermarket stuff) and did the laundry now, did not believe it.

And what was wrong with Robbie? He never went over to Brett's anymore, even though the hills were great for sliding, just stayed in his room with Tofu. After school he would always take a rest, and when he woke up, he would constantly talk to his cat. Tony could hear him day after day, Tofu this and Tofu that. He was on his cell phone with Brett sometimes, but after a five-minute conversation would quit and need to rest. And what was this thing he mentioned once about pressure in his head? Tony made an appointment with Doctor Janes, the pediatrician, but it was a week away.

Then Tony woke up one night at two a.m. and heard Carol vomiting in the bathroom. He hurried to her and she said, "I'm worse. I don't know what I have, it's not related to the accident."

"We'll go the ER," Tony said.

"No," Carol said. "Not now, I just want to sleep."

"Are you sure?"

"I'm sure. I just need sleep right now."

"First thing in the morning then," Tony said. "I'll cancel my appointments."

Carol had woken Robbie too from a stream of nightmares: people caught in a tidal wave, others trapped in a burning house, his mother dying—which is when he woke up to her retching. He lay there thinking, *Poor Mom!* But no doctors can help. The Wolf will not let them help. He thought of it there in his closet working its poison, but what could he do about it? "Oh Tofu," he said. "I feel so terrible."

And now even Tofu seemed different. She didn't want to lie with him anymore or sit on his lap. The cane is behind this too, he thought. I should never have taken it from Grammy, but she wanted me to have it so bad...

He lay there feeling totally wiped out, then heard his mother vomiting again.

"Mom, Mom, Mom," he said to himself. And then he began to sob.

ROBBIE

IN THE MORNING, IT snowed and school was called off. His father bundled his mother into his car and they drove away into the storm.

Still in his pajamas, he put more wood in the fireplace and tried to eat some cereal but had no appetite. How could any doctor help? It wasn't a disease.

How could anything help? He felt so tired, so terribly tired, and thought of going back to bed. "Tofu," he said, "come here."

She had been here just a few minutes ago but was now nowhere in sight. How had she disappeared like that?

He checked all the downstairs rooms and the garage but didn't find her, then went to his bedroom.

Tofu wasn't there, or in his parents' bedroom, or his father's study. Puzzled, Robbie got dressed, then looked out the window at the snow, which was coming down steadier now.

And there…was that Tofu? Standing out by the road? It was! What was she doing out there and how did she get there? Why wasn't she coming back to the house and begging to be let in?

Frowning, he hurriedly went downstairs again and put on his jacket and hat and boots. *Something is wrong with Tofu,* he thought, *and I know why.*

When he opened the storm door the wind hit him hard, made him catch his breath. He could feel his asthma deep in his lungs. The cold was bad for it, real bad, and he had to get back inside as soon as he could. He trudged through the thickening snow toward the motionless cat. "Tofu," he said, "come here, you don't want to be outside!"

He came closer and closer to her, and suddenly she took off—toward the lane that led down to the cabin. "Tofu, no, don't go down there! There's fishers there!"

But the cat paid no attention and started to run—toward the river, and had to be stopped! He had no choice but to try to catch her, and so he ran.

He could see her ahead of him in the lane and he called out, "Tofu! Come back!" The cat stood there a moment just staring at him then turned and took off again.

"Tofu! No!"

Robbie started to run again. He felt pains in his chest now and started to wheeze. *The Wolf is trying to hurt me,* he thought. *I know it, I know it! It's trying to hurt both Tofu and me!*

The cat kept running and Robbie kept running but much more slowly now. "Please come back!" he hollered. "Please!" But his voice was muffled by the storm.

He could see the cabin ahead in the swirling snow, and saw the green car. There were lights in the cabin, he wanted to go inside and get out of this cold but he had to catch Tofu. The river was frozen now but he'd heard of people going on it, hitting a thin spot and falling through into the deadly water. He had to get Tofu before she reached the river, just had to! But the wheezing was terrible now and he thought that he couldn't go on; he would have to stop. As he passed the cabin, he said to himself, "I can't stop. I have to save Tofu, I have to!"

He ran, and a voice was propelling him forward: *hurry hurry don't slow down run run save cat go out on ice* and he suddenly thought, *It's trying to kill me!* but now he couldn't help himself. *Run run not far now run* and the river appeared in a haze of snow but Tofu kept going, going…

JEFF

JEFF STOOD AT THE kitchen window and watched the snow fall, flakes of peaceful white silence.

He needed to leave here today because of commitments at home, and soon, before the snow turned heavier. Tomorrow someone would come to drain the pipes and clean the wood stove and put other things in order—and inherit what was left in the fridge and freezer.

Sandra had visited two more times, and the second time she had urged him to shave off his beard. "It makes you look so old," she'd said, and he had agreed. And once it was gone, she agreed that his face looked strange, as if his chin had receded. But enough of pretend bohemia, enough of Santa Claus.

He'd be sorry to leave this place but would probably never come here again. It was almost a bit *too* quiet and he really couldn't stand more bouts of questioning himself. But the thing of it was, despite the distractions, he'd worked well here and changed in a positive way. He still hadn't finished the book he was writing because of that short story stint, and he still couldn't see what the ending might be, but it was worth all that to be moving toward something different. He wondered if he would ever tell the owner about those visions he'd had. Probably not, he might think his cabin was haunted.

He'd had no migraines for almost a week and no visions. Maybe "Richard" really was gone for good since he'd done his job. But at home there would certainly be more migraines and that would tell the tale.

He watched the snow fall faster, faster, feeling tremendously calm.

Then he suddenly saw something run past his car. An animal. A cat? Headed toward the path to the river. And then—he could scarcely believe it—a child. A boy, pursuing the cat? In this storm! Was he out of his mind?

He hurriedly put on his coat and hat and went outside. He ran down the path and saw the boy ahead through the quickening snow.

"Hey!" he yelled. "Stop! What are you doing?"

The boy paid no attention to him, didn't seem to hear.

He ran faster and gained on the boy.

Then the river appeared. *Good god*, he thought. He put on a burst of speed, and after a minute caught up to the boy and grabbed his jacket's collar.

"No!" the boy said. "I have to save my cat!"

"Forget the cat, you can't go out on the river!"

"Let me go! Let me go!"

"I won't, you're coming with me!"

"No!" said the boy and fought like mad. "You're not my daddy, you're a *stranger*, you can't tell me what to do!"

"Oh yes I can!" Jeff said, and dragged the kicking screaming boy back up the path.

They reached the cabin but didn't stop, kept going out to the road. "You're going to go into your house and get warm," Jeff said, and the boy was crying now. "I want my cat," he said, choking on tears.

"Your cat will come back soon," Jeff said.

"You don't know that!"

"Oh yes I do!"

Jeff dragged the boy up the concrete walk and opened the storm door and heavy front door and entered the living room. He said, "You stay right here! Right here, you don't go anywhere!"

The boy had covered his face with his hands. He was wheezing hard, fighting for breath.

"Your breather. Use it now."

The boy, still sobbing, started upstairs to his room.

Jeff said, "I'm going outside to watch and see that you don't go anywhere. If you do, I'll catch you again."

ROBBIE

ROBBIE WENT TO HIS room and used his breather. But it wasn't helping at all, and now he was mad. The Wolf! It had caused all this! He didn't care what Grammy said, Mrs. Carney was right! She was right, the cane was evil!

He went to his closet and grabbed it and took it downstairs. It was buzzing hard, was actually hurting his hand, and he threw it onto the living room floor. He angrily put more wood on the fire and shouted, "You hate my mother, won't let her get well, and now you hate me! You made my Tofu run away! You won't help my father stop drinking!"

The fire was burning wildly, brightly, hotter than ever before. And now when he grabbed the Wolf again by its wooden shaft it was suddenly very heavy and tried to bite as he dragged it to the fireplace. It was saying *"No! No! No!* in his head but he shouted "Yes!" and with all his strength he lifted it and threw it into the blaze.

A sudden flash of blinding light and a terrible animal smell. Then a bone-chilling howl filled the room, and then there was only the sound of the crackling flames. And thoughts filled Robbie's head with *no you can't I want bad boy you killed* and then they stopped. And the cane kept burning, burned and burned until it was nothing but ash.

He sat on the couch and watched the flames die. He was breathing easily now and the pains in his stomach were gone. But where was Tofu? Tofu!

Then his parents came into the mudroom, kitchen, dining room, the living room, and his mother was smiling.

His father said, "Robbie, you won't believe it. Mom got amazingly better right in the car. When we left the clinic she didn't feel good, but after we drove for a while she felt terrific, both her stomach *and* her leg." He frowned. "Robbie? Are you okay?"

Robbie was staring at the fire. "I'm fine," he said. "The voices are gone."

"Voices?" his mother said. "The ones you talked about before?"

"Yes, the ones in my head. The ones I told you about but I think that you didn't believe me. And you know why they're gone? Because I burned the cane."

"You *burned* the *cane?*" his father said. "Why in the world did you ever do that? It was worth...god only knows how much."

"Valuable things must be destroyed sometimes. Aunt Lillian told me that."

His father looked flabbergasted. "I don't understand. You went to all that trouble to get the cane back when I pawned it, and now you do this."

"It had to be destroyed," Robbie said. "It had evil spirits."

His father took a huge breath and let it out. He was quiet a minute then said, "Well maybe we're better off just rid of it, we won't have to deal with that nonsense anymore."

"We *are* better off," his mother said. "Don't you see? When Robbie burned it, that's when I began to feel better."

"And I felt better too," Robbie said.

"You don't actually think…" his father said.

"It held us in some kind of spell," Robbie said. "And now it's gone."

"Some kind of spell," his father repeated, then laughed. "That is so Old World, how did you ever come up with it?"

"It's true!" Robbie said. Then he suddenly heard a scratching sound outside the front door and ran to it and threw it open. "Tofu!" he cried, and opened the storm door. The cat came barreling in, covered with snow, and yowled and went right to the hearth.

"Tofu ran away," Robbie said, "down the gravel lane and the path to the river and I ran after her, and a man ran behind me and grabbed me and brought me back here. And that's when I knew that I had to burn the cane."

"What man?" his mother said. "The one who's been using the cabin?"

"I guess."

"We don't know him at all, not even his name," his father said.

"I hated it when he grabbed me, I kicked and screamed but he wouldn't let go. And he said that my cat would come back on her own. He was sure she would."

"And he was right," his mother said. "We'll have to go see that man and thank him."

"We will," Robbie said. "We will."

He slept extremely well that night and heard no voices at all. In the morning the sun was shining and everything sparkled with snow.

In school he said to Brett, "I burned the cane."

Brett's eyes went wide. "You *burned* the *cane*? Ga*zorp*! The golden handle too?"

"I did. I had to. It was evil."

"Yes, it was. It helped me some but hurt me too."

"My dad went through the ashes for the handle but he didn't find a thing. No gold at all."

"It just disappeared? Like that awful bird disappeared?"

"I guess. What did that bird want, anyway?"

"I don't know," Brett said. "Maybe it wanted to tell us something."

"But it didn't talk, like Grip."

"Maybe it was just hungry and thought we'd feed it."

"Maybe so."

"Do you think the cane's spirit survived?"

"I thought you didn't believe in spirits."

"Well maybe I do, in living things, but I don't know about canes."

"Let's just forget it," Robbie said. "I don't want to think of that kind of stuff anymore."

"Okay," Brett said, "we won't. But guess what. I feel good, as good as before I killed that bird."

"I feel good too, my breathing is fine. And my mom feels good and so does my dad. I'm glad we don't have the cane anymore."

"So we can go sliding today after school," Brett said. "The snow is perfect for that."

"Sure is."

"Did you thank that guy for saving you?"

"Me and my dad went down the lane when the snow stopped but no one was there. And the car was gone. But you know what?"

"What?"

"I think I know that man. I never really saw him before he grabbed me but somehow I think I know him."

"You do?"

"I do. Somehow he's not really a stranger."

"Ga*zorp*! Do you think he will ever come back?"

"He might," Robbie said. "We'll just have to wait and see."

www.ingramcontent.com/pod-product-compliance
Lightning Source LLC
Chambersburg PA
CBHW060326260626
47160CB00007B/2694